Florida Heat

By

Jody Vitek

Published by
Satin Romance
An Imprint of Melange Books, LLC
White Bear Lake, MN 55110
www.satinromance.com

Dedication

This book is for my best friend Tracy. You inspired me to finish my first story and made the concept of this book possible. Thank you for being my best friend and supporter.

With thanks to my family and MFW for their years of support, Liz for her fresh eyes and most of all, my critique group: Brenda, Terri, Joyce, Jude and Christine, for their constructive criticism and pushing me forward.

Thank you to my editor, Jane, for making my first time with edits a dream and being patient with my questions. Most of all, thank you for taking the time to make *Florida Heat* the best book it could possibly be.

Acknowledgments

I must acknowledge Brian of Tabara Racing, TCPBA; Carrie of Offshore APBA of Operations, 2001 and Dennis, Predator racing team, 2001/2002. Thank you to Yvonne and Shannon for your medical advice and Lisa for her horse expertise.

Chapter One

Austin General Hospital would be short a nurse today. Maggie Nash went to bed last night with more than a fever, thanks to her best friend Chloe Atwood who had been kind enough to share her flu germs. She opened one eye then the other. Red glowing numbers pierced the darkness like a black cat's eyes in a dark back alley.

Heavily lined drapes over a room darkening shade covered the windows, keeping any light from streaming in. Her eyes adjusted, and she strained to see the clock—two-seventeen in the afternoon. Her husband Mike would be working at the hospital pharmacy for another three hours. She wondered how he was holding up since she disturbed his sleep on and off all night. He had asked if he could do anything for her. But when you're sick with the flu, there's not much anyone can do that would help.

Legs stretched and bent, along with her arms, as though she were Frankenstein coming to life. Her stomach ached, and her side muscles strained when she sat upright. On the edge of the bed, she slid her feet into slippers, put on her robe and walked out of the room into the peace and quiet of her home.

A thick arm grabbed her around the waist. She screamed and wiggled in the crushing embrace. A leather-gloved hand cupped tightly over her mouth. Her screams silenced. She continued to twist in the intruder's arms. A hand spread from the bottom of her breast to the top of her hip.

Her captor's cupped hand on her face forced her back into his chest. A thick blunt object pushed in at the middle of her back. She gasped and her back arched. A gun?

"Quiet," a deep male voice said. The voice came hushed and furious. "I have a knife. I'm going to remove my hand, and I want you to remain quiet. If you understand, nod."

Bile churned in her stomach. She nodded.

"Good." The intruder paused and removed his hand and arm. "Go to the kitchen. Get the phone."

"The phone? What do you want?" They walked toward the kitchen. She twisted at the waist, trying to see who was abusing her. His hand reached up, fingers pressing into her skull, preventing her from seeing his face.

"Don't turn around. Straight ahead."

Her esophagus became a backed up drain pipe of stomach bile. "I can get you money if that's what you want."

"Tempting, but that's not what I'm here for. *You're* not supposed to be here."

She snatched the portable phone from the cradle.

"When's Mike getting home?"

The vomit rose in the back of her throat, and she dashed for the sink.

"What the…?"

Her head was over the sink, misery audible with each heave of her stomach.

"Jesus." His body heat radiated warmth; he stood that close. "Don't run again. You'll regret it." Light glinted off the knife blade now at her waist.

"Fine. Next time I'll puke on you."

There would be no escaping the horror she found herself in.

Once her mouth was rinsed out and her face wiped, she held onto the counter for support.

He grabbed her arm and repeated, "When's Mike getting home?"

"You know Mike?"

"I'll ask the questions. Got it?" He pushed her toward the kitchen chair. "When?" he questioned with force.

"Three hours," she quivered, falling onto the chair.

Although rape was no longer a credible threat in her mind, it didn't make the situation any better. This man was serious. But what did Mike have to do with it all?

Maggie wrapped her arms around her waist, hugging herself, and rocked back and forth. Clenching her legs together didn't stop the out of control jiggling.

"I want you to call Mike and get him home now. Not a word about me."

Her captor stood behind her, watching, as she pushed the phone buttons.

"This is Maggie. Is Mike available?" Another pharmacist answered, placing her on hold. Her legs bobbed, and her eyes burned as she closed them.

Mike came on the line. "Maggie, what's wrong?"

"You *need* to come home." Her throat tightened. "I'm not feeling very well."

"Honey, you know I can't come home just because you're sick."

"It's more than not feeling good. Something's wrong."

"What? What's wrong?"

She heard his concern. The knife blade poked into her side. "I can't get into it over the phone." She cried out, "I *need* you to come home."

"Hold on."

"He put me on hold." She glanced at the blade and swallowed hard.

The man remained behind her, and she still hadn't seen his face. An offensive lineman's hand rested on the edge of the table though. Thick and large. Warm breath fell upon her ear. Too close again.

"Nice work." He pulled the hair binder holding her long blonde hair on top of her head, releasing the hair to fall down her back.

She shivered. To distract herself, she looked at the pictures on the wall. A figure reflected in the glass.

Mike's voice came back on the line. "Maggie I'll be there as soon as I can. Do you need to go to the doctor?"

"I don't know. I don't know." Her reply came unsettled.

"I'll be there as soon as I can. I love you." Mike spoke softly and with meaning. Her heart swelled with the endearment. She hung up and placed the phone on the table.

"Is he on his way?"

"He said he'd be here as soon as he could." She focused on the picture in front of her. The glass could reveal who this man was. But the house was too damned dark with all the shades closed. She could only see a shadowy figure. *Damn!*

"Well, I wonder what we could do to pass the time?" He ran his free hand up and down her arm.

She jerked away.

"I'm not going do anything to you. My boss wouldn't like that. What I want are the drugs, and Mike's going to give them to me."

"Drugs? What are you talking about?"

From the reflection in the picture glass, he twirled the knife in his hands. "I'm here to collect a supply he hasn't delivered on."

Again, she asked, "What are you talking about?" What was Mike doing? This new revelation had her heart racing as though she were on crack.

"The spouse is always the last to find out." A deep-throated laugh came from behind, and the knife was back to her side. "You don't have to worry."

She flinched with his warm breath on her ear.

"When I get the drugs, I'll be leaving."

Ten minutes later the garage door whirred. Mike was home. Maggie turned toward the door.

"Get up. We're going to meet him."

Her heart raced as she obeyed her captor's order. They neared the door to the garage.

"Keep quiet," he commanded. His right hand with the knife slid to her neck, and his left arm tightened around her waist.

The door opened. Her stomach cramped, and the shivering went out of control.

Mike stopped like a Mack truck hitting a mountainside. His facial expression changed from concerned-caring-husband to what-the-fuck in a miniscule of a second.

"What the hell is going on here, Rick?" Mike shouted, still in his white pharmacy coat. "Dammit! I didn't want Maggie involved."

Maggie couldn't believe this. Her captor had a name. And Mike knew it. How involved was he? And to put them in danger like this?

"She's already involved. The boss wants his stuff."

"Well, Maggie isn't what you want." Mike's pitch went up. Was that anger or fear that drove his voice to sound like a girl's?

"The boss wants the drugs you promised, so he sent me to find them. Instead, I find a pretty young thing waiting for me." Rick gave her a squeeze, and his hand ran over her ribs and up to her breast.

Her stomach lurched, and she gagged.

"Listen, I don't have it." Mike stepped forward. "I'm still working on getting it, and she's not a part of the deal." There was desperation in his voice she'd never heard before.

"That's not what the boss wants to hear. He wants me to bring him the goods. Maybe I should bring him some collateral?" Rick's hands played with her midriff.

She gagged again, and Rick stopped feeling her. Her head felt like someone was bouncing a basketball inside her skull.

"She's not collateral for the taking." Mike lunged at them.

The smooth, sharp blade sank into the soft, delicate skin below Maggie's left ear and sliced to her chin. Numbness. Warmth. Then pain. Searing pain.

Like a newborn foal with legs unable to keep her upright, she collapsed to the floor. Her head spun as though she had stepped off a merry-go-round.

Warm liquid ran down her neck. She placed a hand under her shoulder to ease herself upright, but it slipped away from her. Blood. Her blood. Blood ran down her face and pooled under her head.

Her vision blurred. Her world went gray.

Maggie closed her eyes, but they fluttered like a frightened bird. Her body shook. She knew she'd die.

Mike pushed around Rick and dropped to her side. He didn't move her though. "What did you do?" he yelled.

"You got what you deserved." Rick's voice was calm and dripped with spite.

"Maggie, Maggie, can you hear me? Stay with me, honey."

Her body was cold.

~ * ~

"Maggie, you're okay. We're at the hospital." A familiar voice.

Her eyes played peek-a-book with the light. She lay in a bed, yet she knew it wasn't her own. And her body. Her body light and numb, not feeling like her own either.

Her eyes, now open and aware, adjusted. Aware of the circumstances surrounding the situation. Aware of her husband's deception. Aware that life as she once knew it was over.

She glanced around the white room at the familiar faces, looking for the voice. There he sat at the edge of her bed, holding her hand. She tried to yank her hand from Mike's, but instead she watched a slow, drug-induced corpse hand crawl freely across the blanket. The words she wanted to scream at him wouldn't come either. Pain pierced the base of her skull with a ringing in her inner ear.

Her heart had been broken and shattered on the kitchen floor of their home. Their home was no longer *their* home.

She turned and saw her mother, Caroline Carlisle. A minor relief. Caroline smiled. Had she seen Maggie try to smile through the pain and bandages?

"Honey, it's all going to be okay." It was his voice again.

Her head moved slowly to face Mike, and she pierced him with her stare. How could he possibly think everything was going to be okay?

"You need your rest, dear." Her mother patted her other hand. "Close your eyes. We're not going anywhere."

Maggie closed her eyes at her mother's soothing command.

The day passed in and out of a painkiller-induced haze. If she had any dreams, she didn't remember them. Instead, she was living in a damned nightmare.

Her bandages were changed the following day. She no longer had the hand of a corpse. She could drink liquids through a straw and talk at a low level for minimum time. Anger slowly grew in her like the slow drip from her IV bag.

Her father, Steven, slept peacefully on the small sofa in her room. Snow White sleeping on the dwarf's beds came to mind, and she laughed. Studying her father, the sleeping giant, sadness crept into her thoughts.

This giant of a man gave his only daughter to a man everyone loved and trusted. Mike stole that from her and her family.

The sadness turned to anger, and Maggie made a decision.

"Daddy." Her voice strained in the cool room. "Daddy. Wake up."

His eyes popped open and then blinked. "Maggie?" He stretched his legs and arched his back. Moving from the couch to the bedside chair, he whispered, "Are you okay?"

"I'm fine."

"Don't strain yourself. Do you want to write?" He continued to whisper. She wanted to laugh but that hurt too much.

"No, I'll write when I get tired of talking." She reached out. and he gave her his hand to hold. "Daddy, I want a divorce."

"What? Why?" He raised his voice. Clearly, he saw no reason for such, and she wasn't ready to explain—if ever.

"Daddy, please don't ask me questions right now. Can you take care of it for me?"

"Yes. But I don't understand why."

There was a knock at the door, and Mike walked in the room. "They called me at the pharmacy and told me you were awake." He glanced between them. "Did I interrupt something?"

Her father stood, the puzzled expression he wore seconds ago smoothed away. "I need a coffee. I'll be back shortly."

"Thanks, Daddy."

Mike approached the bed, leaned over and kissed her before she could turn her head. He sat in the empty chair her father left behind. A dwarf now sat in the giant's chair. Worse yet, a coward.

"How dare you kiss me," she hissed.

"Maggie, please. Please listen to me."

She turned away. Hearing his pleas would be one thing, but to see the desperation on his face was another. She had to stay strong.

"I didn't think they'd come to the house. I didn't realize they knew where we lived." He reached for her hand.

She pulled it away, disgusted. "You're stupid and blind."

"You're right. Maggie, the cops are asking questions. I need you to tell them this was a break-in. That we don't know who did this."

"What do you mean *we*? I *don't* know these people. You *do*," she croaked. Maggie hated not being able to yell or scream at Mike. Her body coiled tight.

"You don't know them, but you do know one man's name. I need you to help me right now by not telling the cops anything. I would lose my job, and then what would we do?"

"I'll do this for you, but you need to do something for me." She turned and faced him.

"Anything. What?" The pleading tone remained.

"Stay away from me. I don't want to see you again." The bandages wrapped around her head, as if she had a face lift, prevented Maggie from expressing any feelings with her face. Her eyes would have to convey her feelings.

"What? I won't do that. You need me right now. *I* need you right now."

She crooked her head to the side. "Get out. I never want to see you again." Her voice told him her disgust and contempt even if her face couldn't.

"Maggie—"

"I said get out. Leave now." Tears ran down her cheek. So much for true love.

The trials of interacting with Mike exhausted her voice and body. She was asleep before her father returned.

Chapter Two

Maggie's fingers drummed the steering wheel. Two months had passed since she'd last seen her horse, when she said goodbye to Texas and hello to Florida. The wooden fence came into view, and soon the fence line encountered a rock wall. Bumblebees—very excited bumblebees—danced and bounced in her stomach.

She drove through open gates, under an iron sign reading 'Rolling Rock Ranch'. Big oak trees lined the long drive. The white, black-trim, two-story house with matching barns and buildings had her longing for home.

She stepped out of her red BMW Z4 convertible and ran fingers through wind-tangled hair, brushing the tresses from her eyes. She pulled a large section to the front of her shoulder, covering the scar on the left side of her face.

The thrill slipped a moment with the realization that the last time she had ridden had been with Mike, two days before the accident. *Accident*, if you wanted to call it that. The back of her fingers slid along her left jaw from her ear to chin.

Why did he get involved? Both of their families were wealthy and had plenty of money.

"Hi. Trent Randall, owner of Rolling Rock." The unexpected voice behind her made her jump. He had a western drawl and *damned* if she didn't like the sound of it. Slow and smooth.

From the shadow under the brim of his chocolate brown Stetson, brightness radiated from his blue eyes. Her chest tightened, and sudden warmth consumed her. And it wasn't the Florida heat.

"Maggie Carlisle," she extended her hand and gripped the tanned, calloused hand he offered. "I'm here to see my horse, Blue Bonnet."

He stood taller than her. Dark hair peeked out from his hat. She expected him to be older. Much older. He was maybe in his mid-thirties. A few years older than she.

"She's a beautiful golden Palomino," he said. "I helped get her settled last night. She was happy to get out of the trailer after the long ride from Texas. Let's go see her. I'll introduce you to the foreman. He'll show you around, then we can talk business."

Gravel crunched beneath their feet, walking to the barn. His tattered boots gave her a sense of home and those good ol' cowboys. She couldn't have gotten to his boots without having noticed the fit of his jeans. And the fit was to her liking. They accentuated all the manly body parts.

She scolded herself. She wasn't there to ogle the man's ass. She was there to see her horse.

"Your father asked for a larger stall, so you'll find Blue Bonnet in the last one to the right." Trent gestured as they entered the barn. Only a couple of stalls were unoccupied. "Your drive here take long?"

"About two hours. I drove up from White Sand Key."

"Mostly freeway then." He leaned on the post. "Well, here she is."

"Hey, baby, how are you?" She nuzzled Blue and earned a nicker. She didn't care how foolish she sounded.

The aromas of fresh hay and the faint hint of manure tickled her senses. A wave of nostalgia swept over her, and mist crept into her eyes. As much as she missed home, she would be *damned* if she'd go back. A part of Texas would be in her life now, with Blue Bonnet in Florida.

Rolling Rock would be a good home for the mare. Maggie could come, ride Blue and be herself, with no one judging her because of her face.

"Trent," a deep voice called.

The owner's solid bicep brushed across her shoulder as he turned, sending a tingle from her chest to the pit of her stomach.

"Ms. Carlisle, this is Jake, the foreman."

"Nice to meet you." She accepted his dirty, wrinkled hand. "Please, call me Maggie."

Jake appeared to be in his late forties or early fifties, weathered by the sun, his clothing soiled from working the ranch.

"When you're done showing her around, Jake, you can bring Ms. Carlisle to my office."

Maggie gazed at Trent as he strolled away. His well-worn boots proved he worked the ranch and lived atop his horse.

Jake showed Maggie the tack locker with her saddle, blankets, currycombs and other belongings already in place. They left the stable and made their way past the wash-down racks and washer and dryer to private offices for her use. Telling her the ranch rules and hours completed the tour.

Maggie followed him up a gentle slope, past a fenced-in pool and patio. Jake knocked before he opened the door. "Trent?"

"Come on in, Ms. Carlisle." Trent stepped out from behind a large oak desk. "Thanks, Jake."

She walked through the doorway into the office and brushed her hair forward. A habit she'd acquired in order to hide the scar…a habit she needed to break. It wasn't healthy for her mental healing to continue covering the scar and worrying about what others thought of her because of it.

Wood shelves were filled with books. Pictures of racing boats and trophies covered another wall. Maggie squinted, focusing on one of them. A man resembling Trent wore khaki shorts and a team shirt, far different from what a rancher wore. Also on display were various horse photos with captions under them and a framed magazine cover with Trent next to an American Paint. An aerial photo of the ranch hung among them. The pictures reminded her of her father's office, tugging on her heart.

Two wine colored leather chairs sat in front of the desk. Trent had taken his hat off, exposing short brown hair with a hint of a curl. His eyes, the shade of worn denim, formed creases at the corners as he gave her a cordial smile.

"Please have a seat. This should only take a few minutes." He walked around the desk and sat. "Your father has taken care of the costs. I do offer, for a minimal fee, horse rental if you wish to invite a guest to join you for a ride."

Before Maggie could catch herself, a frown twisted her face, and she shook her head. No guests would be riding with her any time soon. She glanced at Trent, glad to see he was getting a folder so he didn't see her momentary bitterness.

"There's one more thing." He pulled papers from the file folder. "I need you to sign these forms, showing you understand the policies and procedures we have here at the Triple R."

"I can understand why my father chose Rolling Rock, and I couldn't agree more with his decision. Blue is going to be very happy here." She signed the last page. "Can I take her for a ride?"

"Of course, Ms. Carlisle." He opened a desk drawer. "Here's a map of the ranch and the riding trails on the property. Or you can use one of the open fields if you like."

"Please, call me Maggie." She stood and shook his hand. "Thank you." She hurriedly retraced her steps back to the stable.

After a thirty-minute ride, Maggie took time to wash Blue. She hated to go, but with the long drive ahead, she had no choice.

"Ms., I mean Maggie. Did you have a nice ride?" Trent's smooth voice sailed across the lot as she strolled to her car. Warmth spread from her belly to her chest.

"Yes, you have a beautiful piece of land here."

"Thank you. I like to think so." He opened her door and brushed her arm.

She withdrew from his electric energy and slid onto her leather seat.

"Will we be seeing you soon?"

"Not sure. I've missed Blue, but with a friend coming from out of town and my work schedule, I'm afraid I won't be coming as often as I'd like to, for now."

"We'll take good care of Blue Bonnet until you visit again." Trent closed her door. "Don't worry about a thing, Ms. Car—Maggie." He tipped his hat and added, "You have a nice evening now."

She rolled her eyes in the rearview mirror at the man standing in the drive as she drove away. "Why couldn't you make him older or obnoxious? Instead, you make him my age and easy on the eyes." She glanced in the mirror and watched Trent turn around. His bowed legs and nice backside came into view. Like the good ol' Texan boys back home, she missed out on another good guy. Save a horse, ride a cowboy played in her head, and she laughed.

~ * ~

Kevin Shaw couldn't help but notice the tall, beautiful, blonde-haired woman who appeared to be alone as he entered the produce section. She carefully selected her vegetables, looking them over for bruises and blemishes. He shadowed her, to make certain she was alone.

She resembled someone he knew. A long cut on her left jaw line appeared to be healing. When she turned, facing him, he couldn't believe it was her. Mike was out on bond, but Kevin hadn't seen him in the store. Would she recognize him? He continued trailing her.

In the breakfast aisle, she perused the various boxes of cereal. He ran his hands through his hair. Kevin had always made a point to remember the wives of his associates, and Maggie had an unforgettable face and body. She met his height, five foot ten, to a tee. Her skin, caramelized by the Florida sun, left her radiant, and she had beautiful green eyes.

She selected a box of granola, turned, smiled, and left the aisle. He quickly pulled a box of whatever in front of him, before he picked up the trail. To stay inconspicuous, he skipped a few lanes here and there especially the feminine hygiene aisle.

Maggie waited in a checkout lane. He stood for a moment not believing his luck. If she was shopping here, she must live close by. But where? He left his groceries in the basket in an empty check out aisle, and walked through the exit.

Kevin slid onto the car's smooth leather seat and watched the exit. When she did come into view, he scrutinized her every move. She approached a red convertible and he took note of the specialty Florida license plate.

"T-X-G-R-L," he read aloud. "All I need to know now is where you're living, Texas girl."

Once she was in her car, he stepped out from behind the wheel and went back into the grocery store. The refrigerator would not stock itself, so he gathered the groceries he had gotten before and those he had missed due to Maggie's welcomed distraction.

He positioned the bags behind the seats and slid behind the steering wheel once again. He listened as the Jaguar's engine purred to life and dialed the familiar number. He waited for an answer.

"Sergeant Fritz."

"Dale, I need some information." Kevin hoped one of his inside connections at the Sheriff's Office would be able to get what he wanted. He only knew of her past. "Are you busy?"

"Nope. Whatcha need?"

"I ran into someone and am hoping you can tell me where she's living."

"Give me whatcha got."

"Her name is Maggie Nash, but her last name may have changed. She lived in Texas last year. I believe she's living here somewhere on White Sand Key or possibly in Sarasota." He shifted in his seat.

"Where in Texas?"

"Austin area."

"What's her husband's name?" Dale was all cop talk, straight and to the point.

"Michael Nash, he goes by Mike. You'll find him in the system."

"You sound like you're enjoying this?"

"More than you know. Mike is an ex-supplier of mine. He was a pharmacist and his wife, Maggie, a nurse. Let's just say he didn't deliver on time. I sent someone to follow through and unfortunate things happened. I'm lucky Mike, nor my subordinate, whom Mike did snitch on, didn't divulge my name." His heart beat faster with the possibilities with Maggie.

"Do you know what kind of car she drives or a license plate number?"

"She's driving a red BMW Z4 convertible, with personalized plates TXGRL." With the air cooled inside the car, Kevin turned up the fan and adjusted the vents to blow in his direction.

"I'll be expecting the usual. I'll be in touch."

"I might add a bonus with this one. She's worth every Benjamin. Anything I need to know?" Kevin needed to protect his assets. It came with a price tag to keep Dale quiet and working for him. Dale kept him informed of situations within the Sheriff's Office such as search warrants and arrests. Kevin didn't want anything jeopardizing his illegal prescription drug business.

"Things are quiet at home."

"I look forward to hearing from you, Dale." Kevin hung up and smiled the remainder of his short drive to the marina. His future looked bright, *and* beautiful.

~ * ~

Maggie stopped the convertible outside the baggage claim door at the airport. She glanced at her watch. She cut it close. The automatic doors opened, and Chloe floated onto the sidewalk with the charm and poise of a Southern belle. Ralph Lauren sunglasses hid her big brown eyes. Dark chestnut hair, curled to perfection, fell on her shoulders.

Once upon a time, Maggie had the confidence her best friend had, until the mishap.

"Hey." A cheerful Chloe waved.

"Hey, yourself." Maggie jumped from the car and studied the staggering amount of luggage Chloe dragged.

"I don't know if it will all fit." Chloe gave the car a once over.

"I think you're right." Maggie hefted the largest suitcase into what BMW called a trunk. "I guess we'll have to leave some of it behind."

They both laughed, embracing one another.

"I've missed you."

"Me, too." Maggie pulled back. Tears stung her eyes, and she blinked them away.

The trunk closed, and with a little strategy, Maggie situated the other bags behind the bucket seats.

"Well, that's everything." She plopped herself behind the wheel. "Let's go grab some dinner. Where would you like to eat?" She pulled away from the curb.

"How does Bob's Boathouse sound?" Chloe sounded as giddy as a child. "It feels like forever since I've been here, and Bob's is always a good time."

"Perfect, it's right on our way. And they still have great live music, not to mention the best food." Maggie negotiated the southbound traffic to White Sand Key.

"I like the new plates. T-X-G-R-L. Leave it to you to come up with something so smart."

"I couldn't help getting the specialty horse designed plates. I thought 'Texas Girl' was fit for a born and raised Texan."

"They're perfect for you." Chloe paused. "Your mother tells me you're waiting until the cut has healed completely before you decide to see a plastic surgeon."

"What else did she tell you?" Maggie's grip on the steering wheel tightened.

Chloe was the sister she never had. They'd always shared everything—*everything*—no matter what.

"Nothing important. We were talking about my upcoming visit to see you, and she mentioned it, that's all. You don't need to get defensive about it. I'm surprised you want to wait."

"You and my mother know I won't need more surgery unless I choose, and I don't think I do." Maggie glanced toward Chloe. "Or are you saying otherwise?"

"No, I thought...never mind." Chloe shifted sideways in her seat to view the ocean.

"Thought what?"

"I thought you'd have further surgery to try and get rid of it."

"It's healing nicely. The doctors told me I shouldn't need further surgery, and the pink color is fading." This was not something she wanted to talk about. The steering wheel would be screaming in pain if it could from her death grip. "If I were to have the surgery, I risk having a more noticeable scar, amongst other risks. I've been religiously using my healing cream." She pulled the usual section of hair forward, "Plus, my long hair helps cover it." The wind defied her and blew the hair back from her face.

"Maggie, you survived the assault and your divorce." Chloe turned back. "Mike is no longer a part of your life. The scar shouldn't be either."

"He'll always be a part of my life, Chloe." Her voice rose. "I loved him once and because of *his* decisions I'll be scarred. He'll *always* be there when I look in the mirror or touch my face."

Silence fell between them. Maggie released the tight squeeze on the steering wheel, sending a rush of blood to her white fingers.

"I'm sorry for raising my voice." She glanced sideways at Chloe. "I know you're only trying to help, but I want everyone to let it go. When it's completely healed, and I know it'll happen, I won't feel the need to hide it like I do now. Maybe then I won't have a constant reminder of Mike."

Maggie knew if anyone could help her with moving on, it would be Chloe. A sister relationship was a powerful thing. Nevertheless, with her busy work schedule, time spent together would be scarce. Being new at her job, she couldn't request a lot of time off.

"Have you gone on any dates since we last talked?"

"No, and you know I'm not looking." She glanced in the rearview mirror, as a memory of Trent's firm ass replayed from the day before. "I don't want to be bothered with having to tell the story about my drug dealing ex."

With a slight shake of her head, Maggie's attention went back to the traffic.

"Why not get out there and have some fun?" Chloe turned sideways and faced her. "You're blushing. What's going on?"

She looked at Chloe. "Nothing's going on...the sun is warm."

"Just because you go on a date doesn't mean you're going to marry the guy. Tell him only what you want. Lie if you have to. Tell him it happened in a car accident."

She hated how easy Chloe made it sound.

"My focus is on work and getting back on my *own* two feet. Everyone thought I helped supply Mike with the drugs. I'm fortunate to have this nursing job."

"But you didn't help him, and you're working."

"Yeah, I've got a job, but not a place of my own yet. My family's vacation home is nice but not mine." She was thankful her father had arranged for the renters to relocate.

"Have you started searching for a house?"

"I started a list of the things I'd like in a place. There's no hurry. Have you made plans with anyone while you're here?" Maggie gave her friend an inquiring glance.

"I'm catching up with some of my old college friends."

"I'm glad you'll have something to do while I'm working."

With a full lot, finding a parking space at the restaurant proved to be a challenge. Maggie wedged her petite sports car between two hulking trucks.

"I think the last time I ate at Bob's was while you were in college here." Maggie pushed a button and slowly the car's top rose. She flipped her visor down, peered into the mirror, and fixed her hair to cover the scar.

"You look great," Chloe said. "No one will notice."

"Thanks." She stepped from the car, and they made their way toward the entrance.

Boating memorabilia hung from the walls and the ceiling. As they waited for a table, the lights dimmed in preparation for the band. Families, groups, and couples on dates packed the restaurant.

Someone shouted Chloe's name, and Maggie turned in the direction of the voice. A tall, tanned man with sun-bleached blond hair approached them. "Do you know him?" She faced Chloe.

"It's Chad Rogers. I went to school with him." Chloe stepped from the small crowd of waiting patrons.

Chad spun Chloe around in a big bear hug before setting her on solid ground. "This must be Maggie." Chad offered his hand. "Chloe's told me a lot about you. She said you'd be picking her up at the airport."

"Really?" Her knuckles cracked beneath his vigorous handshake. "What has she said about me?" How much had Chloe revealed?

"All good."

"It's nice to meet you." Maggie wiggled her fingers once released from his grip.

"Listen, why don't you two join us? I'm here with a group of friends, and they wouldn't mind if two beautiful women joined the group." He gestured to a large crowd of people behind him.

"We'd love to," Chloe chimed before Maggie could protest.

"You planned this," Maggie scolded in a whisper and peeked past Chad toward the group of people. "You set me up."

"Are you mad?"

"Maybe... A little, but I'll get over it." Maggie followed behind an arm-in-arm Chad and Chloe, not able to take the moment away from her glowing friend.

Chapter Three

His gaze caught Chad returning to the table. Were his eyes deceiving him? His new horse boarder approached with Chad and another attractive woman.

Before Team Seahorse embarked on its big weekend of offshore powerboat racing, Trent, as owner and driver of the team's boat, indulged the group with a night out at Bob's Boathouse. Once the Sarasota Sun Coast Offshore Grand Prix events got underway, everything would take on a more serious note.

"Trent, this is Chloe Atwood, a very good friend of mine." Chad gestured to Maggie. "And her friend—"

"Nice to see you again, Maggie." After he shook Chloe's hand Trent offered his hand to Maggie. For the second time, electricity snapped at their connection. The first time at the ranch, he'd blown it off as being something in the air.

"You two know each other?" Chad and Chloe said in unison and glanced at each other.

"My horse is boarding at Mr. Randall's ranch."

"Please, call me Trent." He released her hand and let it slide from his hold. "Would you ladies like to join us?"

"Hope you don't mind. I already offered," Chad interjected.

"Please enjoy yourselves," Trent offered, with a motion to find a chair at the table. "Chad, why don't you make the introductions?" He had trouble averting his eyes from Maggie. She wore casual dress clothes versus the riding clothes she'd worn when they'd first met.

Maggie kept conversations short and played with her long blonde hair. She would gently pull the front section, with her fingers like a comb, across the left side of her face. Was she nervous? Was it out of habit? Was it because of the scar he spotted yesterday in the barn? It appeared to be fresh, and he was curious.

Trent kept up with the other team members' discussions, while he continued to observe Maggie throughout dinner. She had lightened up, talking and laughing with the guys and their significant others. Her behavior and attitude appeared to be genuine and not an act. How refreshing.

The band had been playing for a while, and patrons filled the dance floor. By the time he'd finished eating, he wanted Maggie to share some of her laughter—and beautiful smile—with him.

"Dance with me?" Trent approached her as her fingers ran through her hair.

"Actually," Maggie replied rising, "I was thinking Chloe and I should get going."

"She and Chad are on the dance floor." Trent took hold of her hand and pulled her onto the floor. "Let's show them how it's done."

"I don't feel—"

Before she could say another word, he had her in his arms.

"How long have you lived in Florida?" He stepped in closer and spoke louder to be heard over the band.

Other dancers bumped into them on the crowded floor.

"I've lived here for about a month. What about you?"

"Several years." He raised his voice as the music got louder. "I love it." He caught a floral scent as she moved closer, and there was an ache of an inner longing. She stood tall and upright with perfect posture. In one word...she was rigid.

"Ranching and boat racing make for a strange combination that must keep you very busy. How do you do it?"

"It is a strange combination, I'll admit." Trent smiled and chuckled. "Horses are my first passion. I was raised on a ranch in Colorado. I got into racing for the thrill of the speed. I manage both with good help and great friends."

Chad and Chloe bumped him in the back. Off balance, he gathered Maggie into an awkward embrace. Neither of them moved until she relaxed in his arms.

He knew he shouldn't get involved with a client, a boarder. Not that it was against any rules, but he always thought it best not to mix business with pleasure. Then again, he had never been attracted to one of his boarders. He was entering new territory.

Something drew him to her, and the only logical reasons had to be her beauty and past. To bluntly ask what had caused the scar would be rude. He'd leave it alone and see if she'd bring it up in a later conversation.

"I spotted the racing stuff in your office." She leaned closer to his ear. "How long have you been racing boats?"

"This is our third season. We came close to not being able to race this weekend, but got the engine part in time. Now we can race in our home waters." The dimmed lights changed her apple green eyes dark like a green glass bottle. "What do you do for a living?"

"I'm a nurse at Sarasota General."

"Any particular area of the hospital?" he inquired further to keep their conversation going with the song finishing.

"Intensive Care." The music stopped, and she stepped from his embrace. "I'm sorry, but I think it's time for us to leave. Thank you for the dance."

Trent followed her to the table where Chloe and Chad sat. "Sure you can't stay? The night is still young."

"Thank you for dinner. It was very nice of you. But I need to get some sleep before my shift at the hospital." Graciously, Maggie held out her hand.

"My pleasure," Trent said and took her slight hand again. "Thanks for joining us."

"It's been a long day for both of us," Chloe said, standing next to Chad.

"I'll let you say goodbye and meet you outside, Chloe." Maggie nodded to the others and walked away.

Trent turned back to Chloe. "I hope it wasn't anything I said or did?"

"She's having a difficult time since... Let's just say I'm here to get her back to being her old self."

Trent wondered if it had to do with the scar. While they'd danced, he'd seen it closer than before. However she'd been cut, it was recent.

~ * ~

Trent woke before the sun rose and took advantage of the early hours by going for a laid-back ride on Majestic. While riding, he thought about the day and weekend ahead, glad the boat was ready and running in time.

"So, you think we'll win this weekend?" he asked, and the white and brown Paint snorted. "I think so, too," Trent responded. "Looks like the weather is going to cooperate." He stopped along the edge of the Peace River. "Beautiful, isn't it?" Majestic whinnied and lifted his head.

Trent enjoyed the serene scenic morning from atop his horse as the sun rose. The trees swayed, the river flowed along the rocks, and a crane walked in the shallows as it hunted for its prey. The slight breeze masked the rising humidity they would later encounter.

"Juan's going to be taking care of you while I'm busy at the races." Trent turned the stallion for home.

Horse and rider returned to the barn, and Trent hopped off. He brushed his mount before mucking out the stall.

"Maggie's an intriguing woman. She has some history, and I think she's attempting to hide from it. Or maybe run from it." Trent put the brush away, and Majestic nuzzled him. "Damn that woman's finding her way into my thoughts more and more."

Down across the way he heard a whinny followed by a hoof stomp, and Blue Bonnet shook her head.

"Hey, Blue." He approached her with a chuckle. "You knew I was talking about your owner and had to put your two cents in, huh?"

The mare shook her head and snorted.

"She must be a great rider with a beautiful horse like you." Blue snorted again. "Well kids, it's time for me to get to work."

Trent went into the boat barn and put his hands on the watercraft, hitched up to the team truck ready to go. He gave a silent prayer for their safety and a win before going to the house to grab his suitcase for the weekend away.

He would register for the racing event and check into his room at the hotel, then later meet up with the team to have the boat inspected by the racing officials. Before the block party there would be the parade of boats at six o'clock, where the fans would get to see the boats up close and meet some of the team members.

~ * ~

The parade and socializing with the fans over with, they locked and secured the boat for the night. Trent headed to the block party and before nine o'clock caught a glimpse of Maggie. He had no idea if she'd be there, but hoped Chloe's connection to Chad was enough to bring her downtown.

"Trent, did you hear me?"

"Sorry, Robin. What did you say?" He met Robin after he moved from Colorado and opened for business. As a boarder at the Triple R they had become good friends. Their relationship had never developed into anything more.

"I asked you about maybe going riding soon."

"Not sure."

Maggie had curls in her hair tonight, and it hung past her shoulders. The curls bounced in a playful manner as she walked. His throat tightened, and he swallowed. He couldn't figure out why she had such a strong effect on him when other women didn't.

"Trent, who are you looking for?" Robin scanned the crowd.

"No one." He struggled to keep Maggie, and her delightful curls, in his sight.

"You are, too." Robin laughed and slugged him in the shoulder to grab his attention. "Who is she?"

"Watch it. I need to be able to drive tomorrow." Trent rubbed his arm for dramatics. "I don't know what you're talking about."

"You can't keep up with a conversation, and you're not focused on me. So, who is she?"

"Listen, I'll catch up with you later. Why don't we go riding soon?"

"Later, Trent," Robin laughed as she strolled away.

He caught a glimpse of Maggie at the beer counter, and a team owner, a married playboy, stood in close proximity.

Trent stepped closer and overheard the last of the conversation. Maggie turned away from Scott toward the bar ledge.

"Listen, babe," Scott said as he slid his left arm around Maggie's waist, "I've got a suite back at the hotel. Why don't you and I…"

"I don't think your *wife* would appreciate you being friendly with the guests of Team Seahorse, Scott." Trent tugged Scott's arm away from Maggie.

"I don't have to worry about it since she's not here, now do I?"

"Let go of me." Maggie wiggled as Scott put his hand around her again.

"She's with me, Scott, and *I* don't like how friendly you're being with her." Trent stood between them and faced Scott. He situated his arm under Maggie's and turned her into his left side.

The smell of beer on Scott's breath nearly knocked Trent back. Images of his father and childhood came to mind, unpleasant memories he pushed aside. He held Maggie by his side and was relieved Scott didn't want to fight.

"If you'll excuse us, I'd like to dance with the beautiful lady."

Maggie snatched the plastic glass off the ledge and took several deep gulps of beer. They strolled closer to where everyone danced, and she took another swallow before throwing the quarter-filled glass into a trash can.

"I don't remember coming with you tonight." A little belch escaped, yet loud enough to be heard.

They both laughed.

"Excuse me. I guess I drank too much, too fast."

"It's okay, and you didn't come with me. Just something I said to get you out of there." Glad to have her removed from the uncomfortable situation with Scott, he drew her into his arms to dance.

Tonight, she moved with the style and grace of a princess. Not rigid like the other night. She must've had dance lessons. The color of her eyes captivated him, reminding him of the Balsam firs back home. The smell of her was...he couldn't quite figure it out, but he liked it. Not the same floral scent and not a soap smell either. It was a sweet nutty aroma.

"Would you like to take a walk?" The music stopped. "These functions can get to a person sometimes."

Maggie perused the tables, and he answered her unvoiced question. "She's at the table there." He nodded his head in the direction of the team's table.

"Who?"

"Chloe's sitting with Chad over at that table." He pointed at the table. "Would you like to join them?"

"I..." She stopped short when a man approached.

"Trent, I need to speak to you."

"Excuse me," she said and left to join Chad and Chloe.

After his conversation, Trent located Maggie at the table with Chloe.

"What's going to be exciting to see?" He joined the conversation and placed his hand on the back of Maggie's chair.

"The boat races," Chloe said with excitement in her eyes. "I can't wait for Sunday."

"Will this be your first time seeing offshore racing?" Trent asked Maggie, caressing her shoulder with his fingertips. She sat straighter and pulled her shoulders away from his touch.

"It's Chloe's first time." Maggie glanced up. "I've seen them a couple of times through the years, but it's been a while."

"I'm going for a walk." From Chad to Chloe, Trent's gaze landed on Maggie. "Join me, Maggie?"

"Go ahead. Chad and I are going dancing." Chloe seized Chad's hand, pulled him from his seat, and nearly flipped the chair.

"If you'd like, we can walk the streets or go to the beach. It'd be comfortable along the water with the slight breeze."

"If you don't mind, I'd prefer to stay here. I'm not sure when

Chloe wants to leave."

"She said to go ahead, and she could call or text you when she's ready to go."

"I know, but I'd rather stay here."

"Okay, would you like something to drink? Soda, or a water?" He was pleased to be in her company, but disappointed they wouldn't be alone and away from the crowd.

"I'd love another beer."

He obliged and went to the bar. She's a grown woman, and it wasn't his place to say anything. He wasn't sure how much she had drunk.

"Where's Maggie?" Chloe approached him at the bar.

"Waiting for me at the table. She didn't want to go far, unsure of when you'd want to leave."

"Tell her Chad's taking me home."

"Will do." Trent smiled with drinks in hand and joked with Chad. "Don't stay out *too* late. We've got a big day ahead of us."

"Same goes for you, boss."

Trent raised his hand in acknowledgment and strolled toward the table with a smile on his face. He had Maggie to himself, and he knew how to get her home safe. If she would only allow it.

Chapter Four

"Maggie Nash?"

She turned. "I'm sorry, do I know you?" She gave the stranger a guarded smile. Her throat closed off, and she swallowed. Hearing her married name caught her by surprise.

"You probably don't remember me. I'm an old friend of your husband's." The man grinned and ran his hand through his long black hair. "Are you here for the party or part of the racing events?" He sat in a chair.

"I didn't catch your name." She shook his extended hand with some reluctance.

"Kevin Shaw." He glanced around the area. "Where's Mike?"

"He's not here. We're divorced," she replied monotone. "I go by my maiden name Carlisle now."

"I'm sorry to hear that. Are you living on White Sand Key?"

"For the time being." Cautious, she probed. "Did you work with Mike?"

"In a roundabout way. I'm in the pharmaceutical business and met him on several occasions at conferences." He pulled his wallet out. "Here's my card. Maybe we could have dinner some evening. Catch up on things."

She took the card from him.

"Are you here for the party or with one of the teams?" he repeated his question.

"My girlfriend has friends on one of the teams." She skimmed the crowd, wondering where Trent was with her drink.

"Which team? My company sponsors one of them."

"Team Seahorse." Her leg started bouncing, a sure sign of nerves.

"What does the friend do for the team?"

"I'm not sure." She gave him short answers, hoping he would leave.

"I'd like to get together with you sometime." He placed his hand on her bare upper arm and added, "and talk over drinks."

"I'm busy for the next couple of weeks. I don't know."

"Excuse me," Trent said, handing Maggie a beer, "your drink."

She smiled, took a gulp and released a quiet burp. Trent smirked at her, and she laughed on the inside.

"Kevin... Nice to see you," Trent said, subdued.

"Trent." Kevin nodded.

"You two know each other?" Maggie's head bobbed between the two men.

"As I told you earlier, my company sponsors a team. Sometimes I go to the races, and I've gotten to know several of the other teams." Kevin turned to Trent. "Trent is also well known in the state for his horse ranch."

"If you'll excuse us." Trent extended his hand to her. "We we're getting ready to leave."

She accepted his hand, stood close by his side and took another guzzle of beer, hoping to calm her nerves.

"Good luck at the races, Kevin." Trent glanced at Maggie and back in Kevin's direction.

"Thanks." Kevin flashed a grin. "Maggie, hope to talk soon. You have my number. And if you talk to Mike...tell him I said hi."

"I will." Why did he have to mention Mike's name in front of Trent? Her stomach retaliated against the beer.

She held tight to Trent's hand as they walked away, and her other hand squeezed the plastic cup.

~ * ~

Concern in Maggie's eyes made Trent question *who* this Mike was.

And the way Kevin kept his eyes on Maggie, undressing her, made him leery of Kevin.

"I'm sorry, but I'd like to find Chloe so we can go."

"Chad's bringing Chloe home, but don't worry, I can give you a ride."

"I can drive myself, thank you."

Between the death grip and daggers, Trent knew he had to approach this carefully. "I don't mind, and you wouldn't want to be…"

"I'm *fine* to drive. I won't get pulled over." She weaved through the crowd.

Where was she leading him?

"Maggie, I would rather drive than have something happen to you," he said sincerely.

"I'm not leaving my car in town."

"You don't have to. I'll drive you…"

"And how do you plan on getting home?" She stopped on the sidewalk in the crowd and faced him. People dodged around them.

"I'm staying in town so I'll call a cab."

"Fine," she said with a hard sigh and led him out of the crowd. "Let's not make a scene. Can we leave *now,* please?" She tossed the half-filled cup in the nearest garbage.

~ * ~

Maggie sat in her car's passenger seat and gave him directions while he drove. Frustrated by not recognizing who Kevin was, she remained silent. She couldn't remember ever meeting him.

"Maggie, are you okay?" Trent rested his hand above her knee.

She glanced at her leg. Her stomach knotted at the comforting warmth of his hand. "I'm fine. My driveway is the next one on the left."

He found the garage door opener on the visor, pushed the button, and pulled into the garage.

Before she realized it, her car door opened. "Thanks, but you didn't need to," she said hushed.

"I wanted to." He offered his hand to help her from the car.

"You've been very quiet the entire way home."

"I'm fine. Thank you." Maggie took the stairs up to the back door of the house and turned to find Trent behind her. Her heartbeat quickened. She turned away, not trusting herself. She knew there was a chance of running into Trent at tonight's block party, but Kevin and her past had been unexpected.

Flustered, she opened the door and stood within the threshold. "Thank you for bringing me home." Her voice shook. "You must have an early start tomorrow. I had a very nice time this evening."

"It's still early. How about a walk along the beach?" At her hesitation, he added, "It's a nice evening. Why not enjoy it?"

Maggie turned on the hall light and let him enter. Chloe should've been there to prevent the intimate setting.

"Does this mean you'd like to go for a walk?"

"I'm sorry." She closed the door. "Yes. Did you want something to drink?" Her throat became parched. There was no denying her interest in Trent. And his eyes. She saw and felt his sincerity when he touched her leg in the car.

"I'm fine thanks. Nice place." He reached into his pocket and pulled out his cell phone. "I'm going to call for a cab to be here at eleven-thirty. That should give us enough time for a walk."

She went into the kitchen and got a drink of water, while watching him glance around the house as he made the call.

"Do you live here alone?" he asked putting his phone away.

She nodded, swallowing a sip of water. At the patio door, she slipped off her sandals. "You can leave yours here, too, if you'd like. The sand is so soft and cool I prefer to walk barefoot."

"Good idea."

On the deck, while he took his socks and shoes off, she gazed at the never-ending ocean the full moon illuminated. Eyes closed, she took a few deep breaths and made an effort to relax. She turned at the sound of the door sliding closed, and gazed into Trent's eyes.

They glistened like sapphires in the moonlight and mesmerized her. Earlier in the day, in a well-lit room, his face had appeared tired and worn from the sun and wind. Here, she could only see, and touch, a soft, soothing face.

Maggie pulled her hand away. "I'm sorry..." She shifted her position in the direction of the stairs. "I didn't mean…"

"Don't apologize." He walked with her to the white sand. "I like the way your hands feel." He slid his hand into hers, intertwining their fingers. "Are you upset about what happened in town? You've been so quiet."

She didn't let go; his hand spread immediate warmth throughout her body. It had been awkward to be around Kevin because of his connection to Mike, but Trent gave her a sense of security.

"It wasn't anything." She swore he could wrap his large hands twice around hers.

"How do you know Kevin, and who's Mike?" he asked with caution.

They took a number of steps before she answered. "Mike is my ex-husband. Kevin said he was a work associate of his. But I don't remember ever meeting him before."

"How long were you married?" Trent stopped.

"Long enough to know it won't come easy again." She faced him.

"That doesn't answer my question." Tender with his prodding he asked, "How long?"

"Does it matter?" She pulled her hand free and set off again down the beach. Tears came to her eyes. "It's over." She quickly wiped her face. "He's out of my life for good." This was the one reason she didn't want to be involved in a relationship. She didn't want to explain her life's failures and mishaps.

He caught up to her but didn't take her hand. Oddly, she missed the warmth and feel of his hand wrapped around hers.

"I'm sorry. I didn't realize the subject was taboo."

After an awkward silence, she whispered, "Two years. We were married for two years."

"How long have you been divorced?"

"A month. End of May." No hesitation would ever come with that question. "What about you? Have you ever been married? Any children?" Maggie swiped at the remaining tears.

"No to both. Do you miss Texas?"

"I miss some of it." She stopped and faced the ocean. "But this feels like home to me, too." Yes, this was home.

"How is this home?"

Maggie closed her eyes and released a breath. His body radiated warmth against her back as he stood behind her, sending a wave of heat through her body. She opened her eyes and gazed over the water.

"Growing up, my family spent a lot of time here. My brother and I grew older and went on with our lives. My parents quit using it as often as they had."

"What do you miss about home?"

"The people, but Blue's here now. It means a lot to have her here." She smiled at the thought of her horse. "I missed not riding because I find it very relaxing." She turned and initiated the walk back to the house.

He strolled alongside her, and she accepted his hand.

"Will you be watching the races Sunday?"

"I work during the day and don't know what Chloe has planned." Chloe would be her scapegoat.

"What do you mean?"

"With me at work, she might've made plans. I'm letting her do her own thing while she's here. I couldn't take time off, being so new in my job, and she understands that. I'm glad she has friends around to spend time with."

"Do you have any friends here?"

"Before I moved here, no, but now I've got a few work-related friends." Their joined hands swayed back and forth.

"So how is it that Chloe has friends and you don't?"

"Chloe went to college here, where as I stayed close to home."

"You must love nursing to work in the ICU." His thumb slowly rubbed, almost in a seductive manner, the length of her thumb before releasing her hand.

"I do. It can be challenging at times but very rewarding most of the time." Maggie reached for the patio door, but Trent stopped, turned her around and gently pulled her into his arms.

"Maggie, come to the docks Sunday after work."

He was too close. She stepped from his embrace and into the house. "I'm sorry, but I'll be coming off a long shift and will need to sleep."

"You sure you can't make it?"

"I'm sorry, but I just can't. Thanks for the invite."

"Well, if you change your mind, you know where to find me." He snatched the socks out of his shoes and shoved them into his pants pockets while sliding bare feet into his shoes.

She opened and held the front door for him.

He strolled close, turned and faced her. "Thanks for the walk on the beach." He kissed her slowly on the left cheek. "I'll talk to you soon."

Maggie stood speechless as he got into the waiting cab. When the cab drove away, she went inside and heard the sound of footsteps. Chloe stood at the breakfast bar.

"How long have you been there?"

"Not long, but long enough to know he's interested."

"Well, I'm not, and if he is, he's wasting his time." Maggie quickly strolled through the living area to the stairs leading to her room. "You and Chad are hitting it off."

"We're just friends." Chloe followed her.

"Then why did you leave me alone with Trent only to have him *insist* on bringing me home?" She let her irritation over-ride her teenage feelings for Trent.

"We decided to go for the more relaxing atmosphere at the beach. Plus, Chad thought Trent would appreciate the opportunity, and I agreed."

"The opportunity for *what*?" Maggie's pitch went up.

"To be alone with you. We both see the way he watches you. And I honestly didn't know anything about him wanting to bring you home. We thought you two stayed at the party."

Maggie turned to Chloe with a grimace. "Whatever. I'm going to bed."

"I invited Chad and the college gang to come over Monday night."

"I wished you would've checked with me," she stated, more annoyed than angry.

"I checked your schedule and thought it would be okay. I can call everyone and…"

"No, it's okay. It would be rude to cancel. Plus, I'm off Monday and, well, you know my schedule. You'll need to get food, because I don't have enough for a party."

"I'll take care of it all. Chad invited the team over, too."

"As the saying goes," Maggie continued ascending the stairs to her room, "the more the merrier."

"Trent could be coming." Chloe's words rolled off her tongue in a harmonious tone.

"I assumed as much, since you invited the team. Good night." Maggie reached the top step of her spacious master suite and fell backwards onto the four-poster bed with a loud exhale.

She rolled over hugging a pillow and peered through the dual sliding glass doors. Her private balcony had a view of the beach and ocean. Many nights she'd go and reflect on her life out there.

Tonight was no different. She got off the bed and stepped into the warm night air. Her hand found its way to her scar. Thanks to Kevin, thoughts of Mike crept in. Her only reason for being leery of the guy was because of his connection to Mike.

"The question is, does Kevin know about the illegal drugs Mike stole from the hospital and his arrest?" She pondered the question, watching the ocean as the waves washed in and back out. The effortless motion soothed her soul.

"Kevin did ask about Mike, wondering where he was, so maybe he doesn't know about the situation. Maybe drinks with Kevin would be all right, and I could get some answers to what he might know."

She turned her reflection to Trent and tonight's walk on the beach. Opening up about her past was unexpected, but it felt good afterwards, a relief of sorts. He had an easy way about him that made her comfortable. Opened her up to trusting. Opened her up to feeling loved. Opened her up to being hurt again.

~ * ~

Trent could smell her in the cab. He lifted the collar of his shirt and inhaled, his nostrils filled with a cherry scent. Damned if he didn't love it. What was this woman doing to him?

One thing for sure, she didn't like discussing her ex. Then again, how much did he like talking about his past? What did Maggie's ex-husband do to her? Kevin's a guy she didn't need to be involved with. She had taken his business card and could find him attractive. With a powerful VP position at Franklin Pharmaceuticals, he has money and she comes from money. Who's he to stop her from seeing this guy?

Maggie's large living room displayed pictures, one of downtown Dallas, several horse pictures, and one of a ranch spread. He would use the Triple R and Blue Bonnet to get closer to her. He only had to get her out there more often to go riding.

He sensed her protectiveness of the past. Should he see her after the weekend events or lay low for a couple of days? Shit, here he'd strived to focus on the team and racing, and along came Maggie to throw a wrench in all of it.

Chapter Five

Parked slightly down the road from her house, but with the garage still in sight, Kevin sat upright watching from his car early Saturday morning. He waited for Maggie to emerge in hopes of discovering where she worked.

Revenge against Mike had been on his mind since he had run into her. Maybe revenge shouldn't be a factor. Maybe get even through Maggie.

When the incident happened back in Texas, he only knew she was a nurse at the same hospital where Mike worked. He wanted to know everything about her, and also in the most sexual way possible.

He slid down on the leather as the garage door set in motion to open. His eyes fixated on the door to see who would leave. His fingers twitched with excitement and his groin became warm and swollen with thoughts of her. God, how he loved a challenge and this would prove to be a good one.

Whoever it could be had already gotten in the car by the time the garage door fully opened. He spotted the blonde hair behind the wheel. With an eye on the car and its every move, he followed the crimson color keeping a distance between them.

The car pulled into the parking lot of Sarasota General Hospital and his heart beat a little faster. "Can my luck get any better? She's still a nurse. Damn, she could be visiting someone."

Kevin's heart leapt as the car proceeded to the employee parking lot and a smile formed on his face. Maggie stepped out of the car and entered the hospital. Although she wore hospital scrubs, she remained pleasing to the eye. He adjusted the crotch of his dress slacks.

Instead of using her to get drugs, maybe becoming involved with her would be better. Wouldn't that send Mister Mike right over the edge, he thought.

He knew someone on the hospital staff that could help him. He'd make a call later. Could she make good on her husband's failure? Kevin left smiling but the smile faded as he thought about the party last night. She left with Randall and they looked very comfortable with each other. *Too comfortable.*

~ * ~

Maggie found a note from Chloe when she arrived home Saturday evening from work. 'Getting groceries for the party—see you when I get back.' After she changed, she turned on the TV and caught the news coverage of the races. The reporter made the comment, "It's NASCAR on water." She nodded her head in agreement. The commentators talked about how the water challenged the racers, and then she caught a glimpse of Trent. Her heartbeat quickened, and she let out a sigh. What was it about this guy?

She stepped onto the balcony and stared at the aqua waters of the Gulf. The variation of water shades represented her life. She touched her scar. White like the sandy shoreline. She folded her arms, leaned against the rail, and looked beyond the shoreline. It was time to move on, like into the middle waters where below things aren't so clear. Maggie shivered as she peered out to the horizon. That deepest, darkest part was her future. She couldn't see below or beyond. She had to live for today. It was time to trust.

Chloe was helping her to move beyond her fear of the social scene. It wasn't easy being so aware and conscious of the scar. Of all people, as a nurse she should be able to move beyond the injury. She wore her hair up and away from her face at work and while running. It was her own self-imposed therapy. This made her deal with others' reactions.

Could she trust another man again after Mike betrayed her? She couldn't help but wonder why money had mattered so much in her marriage. If she let another man into her life, would he be able to love her, not for money?

"He claimed to love me, but look what he did." Maggie touched her jaw with thoughts of Mike.

Downstairs in the kitchen she focused on the door where she'd said good night to Trent. Where he kissed her. She touched her cheek and swore she could still feel the warmth of the kiss.

She frowned.

"I can't believe I let him get close enough to kiss my cheek, let alone close enough to possibly notice my scar." Damned if she didn't like his warm lips and want more of his kisses.

She turned from the door. Why didn't he kiss her on the mouth? What would it have been like to have his soft lips touching hers? Her body reacted in ways she didn't want it to around him, but she couldn't deny the woman coming alive inside.

"I don't need this right now to complicate my life," she complained to the empty kitchen. "I came here to get away. To start fresh. I want some breathing room." Rolling her eyes to the ceiling, she asked, "Can You give me that much? God, why do thoughts of him keep coming up?"

"Who's *he*? And maybe I can help?"

Startled, Maggie turned. Chloe held grocery bags. "No one and you can't help."

"So, you do like him," Chloe said light-heartedly, and smiled. "So why fight it?" She rested the bags on the counter.

"I don't know who you're talking about, but I'm not fighting anything." Maggie pulled bags of chips and pretzels from the grocery sacks.

"Maggie, come on. You used to confide in me."

"You'll always be my confidant." She faced her friend. "And I always hope to be yours." She returned to put groceries away and worked on the refrigerated stuff first.

"So then, why don't you tell me?"

"Tell you what?" Maggie spun around.

"You've been thinking about Trent, haven't you?"

"No. I've been thinking about…"

"Not Mike again." Chloe pleaded, "Please tell me it's not him?"

"Actually, I was." She winced at the partial lie, but she couldn't admit she might be attracted to Trent. At least not yet. She had to figure out her own feelings for him. Mike made a perfect scapegoat.

"Maggie, forget about him. Move on, and if you start with Trent, well hell, why not?"

"Okay, enough. I don't feel like talking about Trent or Mike right now. Have you eaten yet?"

"I snacked a little but nothing with substance. What are you thinking?"

"Let's get these groceries put away and go to the Daiquiri Deck. I could go for a Mai Tai Daiquiri and a good burger."

By Monday evening the house had been cleaned, chip bowls filled, cheese and cracker platters prepared and cups, plates and napkins sat out on the table.

Dressed for the party, Maggie went downstairs and found Chloe holding a beautiful bouquet of flowers.

"Who sent you flowers?" she asked, approaching to smell the bouquet.

"They're not mine. They're yours," Chloe said, with one eyebrow quirked.

"Mine? Who would send me flowers?"

"You tell me. I've been dying to know who they're from. Open the card."

"My parents probably sent them." She pulled the card from the holder.

"So?" Chloe asked anxiously.

The card read, 'Haven't stopped thinking about you and would love to have dinner. Kevin.'

Kevin? How did he know where to send the flowers?

"They're from Kevin," she answered with indifference.

"Who's Kevin?"

"A guy I met at the street party." Keep it simple.

"A guy? Come on, Maggie. Did he just walk up to you and start talking?"

"Pretty much. He recognized me." She put her face into the bouquet and inhaled the delightful, fragrant aroma.

Chloe stood wide-eyed with her mouth slightly agape.

"He knows Mike." Maggie glanced around the room to figure out the best place to set the flowers.

"Maggie, that can't be good if he knows Mike." Chloe rested her back against the counter.

"He's harmless. He knows Mike through the pharmaceutical business. He's a VP for a large company."

"What does he want? Never mind, stupid question."

"I think he wants to get together and talk about Mike." Maggie strolled out of the kitchen with the vase and Chloe trailed behind.

"You're kidding, right? Come on, Maggie, he wants to go out with you."

"Well, I never said yes, and as of right now, I'm not sure if I will."

"Good."

"What's that supposed to mean?" The words came out harsher than she meant.

"I don't think someone who knows Mike is the kind of person you should be going out with."

"Not everyone who is associated with Mike is bad, Chloe."

Sleek raven hair, she recalled, had curled below his collar and eyes as green as her own had radiated mystery and intrigue. He had been pleasant. The other night he'd worn shorts, and she had noticed his tanned muscular legs.

She positioned the vase in the middle of the table and moved a few bowls. "Has there been any response to who'll be coming to the party?" She wanted to bring the party back into focus, curious to know if Trent had replied.

"Some are planning on stopping by, but others decided the weekend was already long enough. Chad didn't say who though."

The doorbell rang, and Maggie opened the door to find Chad with

41

a bouquet in his hands. "The flowers are beautiful." Maggie let him through the door. "Chloe will love them."

"Actually, they're for you. Thanks for letting Chloe have a party." He handed her the flowers and removed a single red rose from behind his back. "This one's for Chloe."

"Thank you." She entered the kitchen to put the flowers into a vase. She could only wonder if Chad had stronger feelings for Chloe than Chloe had for him, something a little *more* than a friendship.

Other friends followed quickly. Soon the music was playing, and people were dancing.

Maggie poured more chips into the bowl and checked the other foods requiring a refill. With nothing needed, she turned, and Trent stood right there.

"Excuse me," she said nonchalantly, and her stomach knotted.

"I was hoping we could talk?" Trent leaned closer to be heard over the music.

"About what?" She continued to glance at the table filled with food and rearranged bowls.

"You, me...or whatever comes to mind."

"What can I get you to drink?" She turned to face him and his crescent shaped blue eyes.

"I'm fine, thanks. Can we talk?"

"Hey Trent, I'm glad you made it," Chloe said coming near.

Saved, Maggie thought, as Chad approached, diverting Trent's attention.

"Hey, boss. Are things all set for the party on Friday?" Chad inquired and placed his arm around Chloe.

"Yup. This year it's a celebration party, too. We've had a great season so far and with our win yesterday, I want it to be big."

"Bigger than last year's?" Chad grabbed a handful of chips from a nearby bowl.

"You bet." Trent turned to Chloe and Maggie. "Chloe, I know you'll be with Chad, but, Maggie, will you come to the party?"

"Yes, we'd love to. It'll give me the chance to see your ranch." Chloe responded before Maggie had a chance.

Maggie sneered at Chloe. She turned to Trent and asked, "I'm sorry, but when is this party?"

"This Friday."

"I don't know. I may have to work at the hospital." Her interest in Trent and Chloe's pushing them together was all happening too fast. Moving forward would happen at her pace and no one else's.

"If I remember right, you're off. So, you'd be able to make it to the party," Chloe stated.

Nails dug into her palms as Maggie clenched her hands. She shot daggers in Chloe's direction. Giving her attention to Trent, she said, "I'm sorry, maybe next time." Where the hell did that come from? Trent beamed with his killer smile. She was in trouble. She knew exactly where it had come from—attraction to the man.

"I'll leave the invitation open. I hope to see you there, Maggie."

"If you'll excuse me, I'm going to check on the other guests." Maggie disappeared into the crowded living room.

She slipped onto the patio and welcomed the slight ocean breeze. The crowded room was warm, and her body betrayed her warming at Trent's presence.

She strolled into the sand, released a breath and wiggled her toes, letting out a quiet giggle. She'd wanted Trent to be at the party, but once he was there, she'd become uncomfortable. She acted like a schoolgirl with a crush. Maybe it was because of not knowing how to react to her unsteady legs or quivering stomach when around him.

She stepped into the darkness as the last edge of light illuminating from the house dispersed.

"Maggie," Trent called catching up to her. "Mind if I join you?"

"It's a public beach. You're welcome to walk on it." He didn't take her hand as he had the other night, and she found it strange how she missed his hand in hers.

"Did I do something to upset you? Because if I have…"

"You didn't do anything wrong." *It's me.* "I needed some fresh air."

"You left the party, and I didn't know how safe it would be for you to walk alone."

"I've never heard of anything happening here. But thank you for thinking of me and my safety again." She didn't care to risk exposing the scar with the breeze and moonlight. To avoid the complex issue of explaining the accident she stayed to his left.

"Again?" His eyebrows furrowed.

"You insisted on driving me home the other night. Remember?"

"I didn't exactly insist. I didn't think you should drive after having a few drinks."

"I was fine to drive. I didn't want to argue in front of the whole city. So, what gives? Why were you so insistent?"

The moonlight softened Trent's face; stubble peppered his chin and jaw. She wanted to reach out and touch him. Feel the roughness of the coarse hairs on her palm.

"I didn't want you driving, plain and simple."

There had to be more to the story, but she let it go.

They walked a short distance in silence when he asked, "Have you been to ride Blue Bonnet lately?"

"No." The mention of her horse put her in a somber mood. "I've been busy working, and I've got another busy work week ahead of me."

"Does it bother you, knowing she's here, and you can't ride her?"

"Of course, but it's no different than if we were still back home. My schedule would still be the same, all over the clock. I ride when I can. Tell me about your move from Colorado. You must miss home."

"I left because the time was right. I searched around, found Rolling Rock Ranch and made an offer on the seventy-acre property the moment I walked the grounds."

"The first time you saw it?" Maggie couldn't believe a person would do such a thing. "You didn't even look at other places?"

"Nope. Knew I'd be happy 'cause I'd be around horses and running my own business."

"I'm getting chilled. We should get back to the party."

"How long is Chloe here to visit?" he asked, still by her side.

"She's here for two weeks. I think she and Chad are growing close, so who knows what could happen." She stayed at his right, praying the wind and bright moonlight would not expose what she worked so hard to hide.

"She's only been here for a short time, and Chad's been busy with work and racing. How could they be growing close?"

"I can tell."

"You know, they say a woman's intuition is right about these things."

"Do they?"

"Okay, so maybe I said that to make an impression." His eyes lit up with laughter.

"And why would you need to impress me?"

"Why don't we let woman's intuition help you decipher that one?" he replied as they approached the house. "I think it's time for me to head home. I have a long day ahead of me, having been gone over the weekend."

He trotted up the deck stairs two at a time and left her standing in the sand. He turned back and smiled. "Have a good night, Maggie." He disappeared into the crowd.

Maggie stood for a moment at the bottom of the stairs. What was he talking about, women's intuition? Oh, my God! Does he know she has feelings for him? Maybe he was the one with the intuition.

Chapter Six

Tuesday morning Maggie came downstairs pleased to see the table cleaned off and no bowls of chips or dip left sitting out. She couldn't make herself sit and watch the coffee brew and embarked on making a sweep through the living room for empty plastic cups and paper plates.

Trent came to mind as she moseyed past the big windows. She stopped and peered at the wide expanse of water. Could Trent be different from Mike? How important was his money and lifestyle to him? Could he love her without it all?

She shook her head, threw away the few cups she found, poured a cup of coffee, and went onto the deck. She finished the cup of coffee with Trent still in her thoughts and decided a run on the beach would clear him out of her head. She left a note for Chloe and after dressing headed outside.

The beach had been freshly groomed for the locals and tourists. Lifeguards opened their stands and prepared for emergencies. With Trent, Kevin and Mike on her mind, she reached her mile mark and still couldn't decide whether to meet with Kevin or not. There was the possibility to learn more about his business relationship with Mike. Maybe seeing Kevin could help her close the door to the past with Mike.

She turned for home and strolled most of the way back. The stingrays swam in the shallow waters along the shoreline and put a smile on her face. She didn't see the dolphins this morning because it was too late. They only came close in the very early morning hours,

46

jumping and playing.

She sat on the deck stairs to relax and heard the phone ring. She jogged into the kitchen and answered, "Hello?"

"Hi, honey. I'm glad you're up," Caroline Carlisle bubbled.

"Hi, Mom." Maggie poured a fresh cup of coffee and inhaled the hazelnut aroma. "It's nice of you to call, but you shouldn't feel as if you need to call so often."

"Honey, your father and I miss you and want to keep you informed on the social events here at home. Are you okay? You seem preoccupied."

"Mom, as much as I enjoy hearing about what everyone is doing, I came here to get away from where it happened. I need time to heal." Maggie stopped herself from yelling the words personally, mentally, and physically. "Don't get me wrong, I do miss everyone."

"Talk to me."

Maggie stared through the picture window toward the Gulf and confided. "Why? Why did Mike throw away our dreams of having a big home, children, and a summer place on the beach? Why did he toss aside my love and our future? Was it all just for more money?"

She stood in front of the window again and sipped her coffee as she wondered, yet again, why Mike had destroyed their lives together. "Why did he think I would love him any less if we didn't have money? We had money, Mom, but apparently not enough for him. I don't understand what I did to give him the impression we needed more."

"Maybe knowing you both grew up having it, and that you'd be receiving a trust fund, fueled his need to show you he could provide for you. We've been through this a million times, dear."

"I loved him. Wasn't that enough?" She turned away from the window.

"Maggie, you can't go on beating yourself up like this. It's part of your past now." Her mother paused. "It's time for you to move on. You have a great job at the hospital. You're living on the beach, and now Blue Bonnet's there. What more could you ask for?"

Maggie looked back at the beach again and thought about it. "But Mike and I planned what I thought was going to be a future for us. We talked about having children, how many, what we'd name them. All the things I dreamt about as a little girl."

Dead air filled the line for a moment.

"Maggie, you'll still have it all. You're still young. You'll find someone...the perfect someone for you."

"I love you, Mom." The cheer tactic had a slight effect, and Maggie snickered.

"What are you laughing about?"

"You made me think of something." Trent. "Chloe had a party here last night with a few friends from college. Something stupid happened." A lie, but any mention of Trent and her mother would get excited.

"What happened?"

"Oh, this guy was sitting on the back of the couch talking to a girl, leaned down to talk in her ear and fell right into her lap." She earned a slight laugh from her mom and asked, "So why were you calling?"

"To say hi and catch up on things. Enjoy your time with Chloe, and I'll talk to you later. Say hi to her for me, too."

Her mother made her feel better without even knowing it. The thought of last night brought the smile back to Maggie's face. Trent didn't have a date last night, at the street party or the night at Bob's Boathouse. He was polite and had manners that would please her mother. So, what was wrong with him?

The way his shirt clung to his broad chest and the fit of his tight, boot-cut jeans made it difficult to forget him. It was a pleasure to dance and talk to him. But did she want to get involved with another man?

The warm coffee cup she held reminded her of the warmth of Trent's big strong gentle hands. A sensation, a zing, ran from her hand through her entire body every time they touched. She could still feel it. This never happened when she was with Mike.

Maggie peered into the rich brown of the coffee and remembered his hair. She'd thought about amusing herself by fingering the curls on the back of his head. He had a wild appearance about him with that tousled hair and the rough start of a beard.

"Money, he definitely has money." Maggie cringed. "Owning the ranch and an offshore racing team proves to me he has money." Money, the one thing she *didn't* want to base a relationship on.

~ * ~

Maggie, Chloe and Chad ate a late breakfast. After Chad left, Maggie approached Chloe while they cleaned up in the kitchen. "Why did you deny there was something going on with you and Chad?"

"What do you mean?" Chloe scrubbed the skillet.

"I asked you the night after the street party about you and Chad. You told me you were only friends, and this morning he came popping out of your room. So, what happened?"

"Things happened, that's all," and she swung the pan in Maggie's direction for her to dry. "Two friends meeting again, older and wiser."

"There's nothing wrong with it." Maggie wiped the skillet dry. "I'm sorry if I implied that. You told me you were friends, and then I see the two of you together and..." Quiet for a moment, softening her tone, she asked, "What are you going to do when it's time to go back home?"

"I don't know. So, maybe wiser wasn't the right choice of words." Chloe stated it plain and simple and headed for the patio doors.

"Have the two of you talked about it?" Maggie was concerned for Chloe and followed, tossing the towel on the counter.

"Chad seems to think we can do the long distance thing. I told him I can't because I've been there before, and it doesn't work." Chloe leaned against the deck rail and focused on the water. "I asked him to call me if he ever came into town, and I'd do the same. I guess you could say he's a friend with benefits."

"And?"

"And what?" Chloe turned to face her. "I have a job and home waiting for me. I can't up and leave *everything* because I decide to have a *fling* with an old friend."

"I know. It's...I can tell you're having a difficult time with this."

"But it's a decision I made, and I'll have to work through it." Chloe turned back to the ocean. "And I *will* deal with it when I leave."

Quiet for several minutes, Maggie asked, "Why did you mention

49

my work schedule after I turned down the party?"

"Because I want you to go." Chloe plopped down in a deck chair. "I don't want you sitting home alone when you could be at a party where a certain host has a very strong interest in you."

"And how do you know he's interested in me? Has he told you or Chad?" She sat on a chair next to Chloe.

"No, but you can see it in his eyes. And he takes the time to be with you."

"When you leave and go back to Texas I'll be sitting home alone. So tell me what the difference would be whether I go or don't go to the party? Plus, you can go without me."

"Well...I'll still be here, and you're my hostess. I would think you'd want to spend some time with me before I leave." Chloe leaned back and folded her arms across her chest.

"Maybe you should think about staying home and sitting around doing nothing with me here, instead of going off with Chad."

"That isn't fair, Maggie." Chloe sat upright and faced her.

"You're right. I'm sorry." Maggie bit her lip and studied her feet.

Silence fell between the two friends.

"Why won't you go to the party with me?" Chloe had leaned back again, with her arms to her sides.

"You know I don't like partying."

"But you made it fine at Bob's, the street party, and the one we had here at the house."

"I know, but it's still difficult for me." Maggie touched her scar and in silence cursed Mike. "I'll think about the party. Okay?"

"Good. Now why don't you be honest with me and tell me how you feel about Trent. I *know* there's something there."

"There's nothing *there* because I don't know the guy," she said with an edge of impatience.

"Yes, you do. You've had conversations with him on several different occasions and one of them was on an intimate level. Maggie, why are you denying yourself?" Chloe placed her hand on top of Maggie's.

"I don't need a man in my life where all he wants is money and he feels that's all I need to be happy. Yes, it helps, but you need to have love, and I don't think Trent has any interest with the love part of the formula." Maggie's mouth ran like a sprinter running a race.

"What do you think he's interested in?"

"Money and sex."

"I think you're wrong about the sex part. He'd have moved on by now and wouldn't be wasting his time to walk and talk to you."

"Look at the ranch and the racing. The ranch brings the money, and the racing brings the girls. He has it all."

"Do you really think that's it?" Chloe sat up again.

"Yeah, I really think that's it, and we'll find out when we go to his party." Chloe wore a whopping smirk, and Maggie realized she'd agreed to go. All of this talk about Trent got her frustrated, had her mouth spitting out words she regretted, and now it was too late to back out.

"Yes! You're going with me to Trent's party." Chloe was up and out of her chair.

"No, wait. I'm not—" Defeated, Maggie sat up, positioned her head in her hands and shook it from side to side. "Don't tell anyone I'm going, *including* Chad. Promise me you won't."

"Okay, I promise I won't tell *anyone*."

Maggie hoped Chloe could keep her promise, knowing it would be difficult for her not to say anything to Chad. She didn't want Trent to know. She wanted it to be a surprise. She wasn't ready to admit there could be something there. Something between them.

"Are you and Chad doing anything tonight?"

"No, but he's coming here for the Fourth of July. You don't mind, do you?" Chloe sat back down.

"No. You know I'll be working. Truth be told, I'm glad you have him and your college friends to spend time with while I'm not here." The phone rang, and she skirted her way around the patio furniture saying, "I'm sorry I can't spend more time with you."

Inside, she answered the ringing phone and gave a cordial 'hello.'

"Hi, Maggie."

"Kevin." She spoke softly.

"Were you expecting someone else?"

"No. Thank you for the beautiful flowers." She peered to the deck where Chloe sat and made sure she couldn't hear or was on her way inside.

"They're not as beautiful as you. I was hoping you were available for dinner Thursday?"

"I have to work." Then reflecting on her conversations with Chloe and curiosity about Kevin, she asked, "What time were you thinking?"

"When do you work?"

"My shift starts at six, and I like to be early. If you want to meet someplace downtown maybe we could make it a late lunch or, in my case, an early dinner." She peered outside again to check on Chloe.

"Why don't you meet me at Bonefish on 41?" Kevin suggested.

"What time?"

"They open at four, plenty of time before you have to work."

"I'll see you there." Maggie hung up and went back outside.

"Who was that?"

"My mother," she said to quell Chloe's curiosity. "She says hello. Why don't we go to the Daiquiri Deck for lunch before I have to leave for work?" Maggie suggested, not giving Chloe the chance to ask further questions and catch her in the lie.

"Sounds good to me."

Maggie snatched her purse, and they left. Lunch would be interesting with Kevin. She anticipated he could tell her more details about his relationship with Mike.

Chapter Seven

Everything was set to go off without a hitch for the big party on Friday. Invitations had been mailed five weeks ago, yet one remained unsent—Ms. Maggie Carlisle's.

Finished with his morning rounds, Trent sauntered to the back of the house, past the pool, and down a slight hill. The flower garden gave him solitude and reminded him of his mother.

She had always tended to her flowers and kept beautiful bouquets throughout the house, a tradition he'd continued once he settled in Florida. His horse or the flower garden always brought him back to Colorado and his family when he searched for inner peace.

Trent reflected on the women presently in his life as he sat alone on the stone bench. His mother had struggled with an alcoholic, abusive husband and used her strength to leave, raising her son as a single parent. Yet they hadn't been alone, because they'd lived with his maternal grandparents. Now Grandma, *there* was a woman. Strong, gentle, kind, she nevertheless gave tough love. Her love had made him the man he was today. He respected women and their worth, never taking them for granted.

Janet, his girlfriend at the time, came along, and he thought he found in her both his mother and grandmother together. Wrong. A Black Widow disguised as a Daddy Long Leg, and long legs she had.

Maggie came to mind, much like a graceful dolphin with tough thick skin scarred by shark attacks. Divorced and scarred by someone—somehow. When he inhaled the delicate scent of the flowers, memories of how wonderful she smelled at Bob's Boathouse inundated his senses.

He made the decision to hand deliver her formal invitation. A verbal invite alone wouldn't do. He needed her to understand how much he wanted her to attend his party. At the wood's edge, he opened the door to the small tool chest and took hold of the cutting shears. He cut four yellow and five white daisy stems, three stalks of each pink and red snapdragons, and put the cutters away before returning to the house. He trimmed the ends, took off low leaves, and arranged them in a mix of size and color.

Chad had informed him about plans with Chloe and revealed Maggie worked the late shift starting at six o'clock. He hoped she would still be at home and made the two hour drive to her house.

~ * ~

Maggie relaxed on the deck with a book after Chad and Chloe left for Sarasota's Fourth of July festivities. She hadn't been able to get Trent's party off her mind and wasn't enthusiastic about having to go. Chloe would hold her to her promise though. Not that the man didn't intrigue her, he did. It was the large group of people she worried about. She knew she couldn't hide from living life because of the scar. It was healing well. She simply had to remind herself of that.

She startled when the doorbell rang, not expecting anyone and thought about not answering it. She peered through the peephole, turned and leaned against the door. Trent. What was he doing here?

He knocked on the door, and she ran her fingers through her hair. She turned around, gripped the doorknob and opened it. "Trent, what are you doing here?" she asked as he opened the screen door.

"I was going to leave this." He handed her an envelope. "You weren't answering." His eyes roamed her from top to bottom. "These are for you."

"You came all this way to deliver an invitation and these flowers?" She accepted the flowers wrapped in newspaper.

"I'm meeting friends and thought I could do this on my way."

"Oh." She'd hoped he had taken the time to make the special trip for her. "Would you like to come in? I should put these in some water."

"Chloe with Chad?" He followed her into the kitchen.

"They're spending the day together." Maggie opened a cupboard in search of a vase.

"Does it bother you she's with Chad when she's here visiting you?" He stood on the other side of the L-shaped counter.

"No, some of her friends from college live in the area, and I knew she'd be spending time with them." She filled the vase with water. "I'm new to my job here so getting time off would be nearly impossible. I'm glad she has someone to be with." She nestled the flowers inside the container.

"What about you?" he asked curiously and slid closer to the end of the counter. "Don't you wish you had someone to be with?"

"No," she stated frankly and stayed behind in the kitchen.

"That doesn't mean you have to be alone, Maggie."

Trent strolled around the counter and closed in on her. Her stomach flipped. His slate eyes had a hint of blue shining through.

Maggie stepped back from his looming figure. He was too close. Her voice quavered. "I'm alone because I want to be...and I'm okay with it."

"Are you afraid of me, Maggie?" he teased as he moved closer to her body.

"No," she squeaked and ran out of counter space.

"Why do you avoid me?" He backed her up against the wall, his hands around her waist, trapping her.

"I don't avoid you." Not about to show her unease with his close proximity, she mustered a firmer voice. "I'm putting a little space between us." Quickly she added, "At least I was *trying* to." Her face felt warm, and a hot wave swept through her belly.

"Why do you need to put space between us? I'm male, you're female, and we're attracted to one another." He smiled suggestively.

"Speak for yourself." She strained to say it firmly, only to fail.

Her knees weakened when her eyes made contact with his dark smoldering eyes. She bit her lip and averted her eyes from his. "I think..." Her gaze went back to him. "It's late, and I need to get to work."

"I hope you'll think again about coming to my party," he whispered into her ear as he leaned close.

Her eyes closed, betraying her, at his slow and delicate delivery of his soft warm lips on hers. She opened her eyes as his lips parted from hers. She stood still against the wall.

He turned before disappearing out the door. "Have a good night, Maggie." He had the nerve to smile, too, showing off those damned dimples.

Maggie didn't move from the wall for a good five minutes. Her heart beat *too* fast for its own good. Her stomach...no, make that her lower region, ached with longing. Unsure how much longer her legs would hold her, she slumped to the floor.

With thoughts about the warmth of his breath on her ear and neck, she glanced at the flowers that sat on the counter and thought of the supple feel of his balmy lips. Her fingertips ran across her mouth, and she questioned what it would've felt like to return the kiss. Her body and mind betrayed her. She didn't know if surrendering to the need would be the answer.

~ * ~

"Where did those beautiful flowers come from?" Chloe asked as Maggie walked downstairs late Thursday morning.

Maggie had arrived home from work in the early morning while Chloe was still sleeping. Today she had her lunch date with Kevin and another long shift ahead of her before having the weekend off.

"Trent brought them," Maggie said as she came around the corner of the stairs.

Last night she'd had a difficult time at work because she found herself distracted with thoughts about Trent...and that kiss. Although soft and simple, the kiss lingered on her lips throughout the night. But when her hand would run across her scar she would be brought back to reality.

"Trent? Trent was here last night?"

"Yeah." Maggie went to the kitchen, and Chloe joined her. "He stopped to drop off the invitation to his party and asked me to think about coming."

"What did you tell him?" Chloe asked excitedly.

"Nothing, he left after he said it." She played it down.

"Left?"

"Yeah. He dropped off the invitation, the bouquet of flowers, kissed me, told me to think twice and left." She poured a cup of coffee.

"Wait a minute. He *kissed* you? How was it? Tell me everything."

"It was just a kiss. Nothing more." Maggie struggled to keep calm and not give in to her feelings. "Where did those come from?" Another vase sat on the dining room table. "Did you get flowers from Chad?"

"No, they're from Kevin. Why would he be sending you flowers again?"

"Kevin?" Maggie found the card and read it silently. 'Looking forward to lunch. Kevin.'

"Come on, Maggie, talk to me. Are you having lunch with him?"

"You read the card?" She placed the card back in the holder.

"I didn't know who they were from and thought they could be from Chad."

"Yes, I'm having lunch with him." She sipped her coffee, not making a big deal out of Chloe having read the card. Her reason was sound, and Maggie couldn't honestly argue with it.

"How well do you know him?"

"Not well, but I plan on finding out how much he knows about Mike and the drug situation."

"He's an associate of Mike's, and that's bad."

"Come on, Chloe. He knew Mike because of the business." Maggie studied the flowers. Kevin had spent more this time. The square glass vase overflowed with purple and blue irises, asters and fillers. Unlike Trent, who brought garden flowers. She smiled at the thought of Trent taking the time to pick flowers for her.

"When are you having lunch with him?"

"Today before work. I thought it would be safer that way. I wouldn't get stuck if I wanted to leave. This way I'll have an excuse."

"Smart thinking. But aren't you moving a little fast?"

"Okay, I'm confused. You're telling me to date and see other men, and when I do, you complain?"

"Point taken."

"I'm only meeting him for lunch...*that's it*. I never said I was dating the man." Maggie picked up her cup and walked away saying, "I'm going to get ready."

~ * ~

It had been years since Maggie ate at Bonefish Grill, and couldn't wait for her late lunch. She wore a linen Capri pantsuit, figuring Kevin would wear a suit coming from work. She applied a minimal amount of make-up, not wanting to under-or over-do it.

"Hello," she said. Kevin waited for her out front, wearing dress slacks and a cotton polo, which surprised her.

"You look beautiful."

"I didn't think scrubs would be appropriate." She lightened the situation, more for herself, with a little laugh.

"Maybe not," he returned with a genuine laugh. He held the door open for her as they entered the restaurant.

The hostess sat them by the front windows. He pulled her chair from the table. A gentleman.

She drank iced tea while he had a beer and found herself unexpectedly at ease with him. The conversation flowed as they talked about her job and touched on his.

"So, what happened between you and Mike?" he asked, taking a bite of his Chilean Sea Bass.

"It wasn't working between us anymore. We both grew in different directions. The divorce was amicable and quickly settled." She was thankful he brought up the subject of Mike.

"Why did you leave Texas to come to Florida?"

"I decided to go for a fresh start." She reached up to fix her hair and stopped herself. "My parents live in Houston but have a home here, which made it easier to move." She took a bite of her Florida Cobb Salad.

"Do you miss home?" He rested against the back of his chair, relaxed.

"My horse is boarded at a ranch in Lake Pine, and her being here has helped relieve some of my home sickness." She smiled at the mention of Blue and because of Trent. "I go riding when time allows." Her guard up on how much to reveal, she didn't tell him the details of names and places. She wanted to give Kevin the benefit of doubt when it came to his relationship with Mike, believing that Kevin wasn't a bad character.

She pushed back her thoughts of Trent and asked, "So how often did you work with Mike?"

"Not often, but enough to remember he was good at what he did." He sat up and positioned his elbows on the table with his hands clasped under his chin.

"How did you remember me?"

"Mike had shown me pictures of you. We also met once at a conference here in Florida. You don't remember?"

"No, I'm sorry, I don't." Was it possible for him to remember her after they met only once? Her stomach quavered with slight unease.

"Understandable. You meet a lot of people at those functions, and if it's not related to your business you don't have a need to remember."

"I guess you're right." Truth in his logic, Maggie relaxed. "I have to ask, how did you know where to send the flowers?"

Kevin received the bill and pulled cash from his wallet before he casually answered. "Online phonebook. It's amazing the things you can find on the Internet." He helped pull her chair from the table, and they walked out together.

"Thank you so much for lunch and the conversation." She got into her car as he held open the door.

"Maybe we could have dinner soon?" He stood within the door.

"I'm sorry, but I don't think that would be a good idea."

"Why?"

"Because of Mike. It makes me a little uncomfortable. Thank you for lunch though."

"We'll talk about this further. Maybe over drinks. I'll call you."

"Kevin—" He closed her door, and she raised her voice. "I can't see you again." He didn't acknowledge her and continued to his car. She decided to tell him later when he called.

Maggie pulled out of the parking lot and headed to work. Kevin wasn't as tall as Trent, but met her height. He wore his hair longer and jet-black versus Trent's shorter, well-maintained brown hair. He had been a gentleman, and the conversation had flowed, so why did it feel so wrong. *Mike.*

The more she thought about Kevin, Trent, and Mike, the more she thought that *maybe* she was being judgmental about Kevin. Not because of Mike, but also because of Trent. She was using Trent as a benchmark of what she would want in a guy...if she were interested.

~ * ~

Maggie entered the house on Friday morning to find Chloe eating breakfast, and she knew the question would follow.

"So, tell me...how was it?" Chloe asked.

"It was very enjoyable." Maggie fixed a bowl of cereal.

"Are you interested in him?"

"I only had lunch with him." She took a large spoonful of granola, temporarily making her deaf to Chloe's questions. The one thing she liked about lunch was getting a few answers. She didn't mind Kevin's company either.

"You didn't answer my question. Are you interested in him?"

She took time to chew, and when Chloe asked again, Maggie heard the irritation in her voice.

"Lunch was very nice." Taking another bite, she went to pour a cup of coffee.

"So, this is a friendship thing?" Chloe asked with a clenched jaw.

She took a sip of coffee and knew the delay with her answers pissed off her friend. "Yes, for right now."

"For right now?" Chloe gawked in disbelief.

"He's a friend, as is Trent. Lunch was comfortable enough, and Kevin made me laugh. It was surprisingly nice. Can we end this conversation? I need to finish eating so I can get some sleep before we leave for the party." She bit into another spoonful of granola.

"I think Trent is *more* than a friend. You've kissed."

"A simple—little—kiss—I didn't engage," Maggie said with a mouthful, not waiting to finish her bite. "He cornered me."

"Maggie, what are you afraid of? Go for it. Have a little fun."

"So it's okay for me to go further with Trent but not Kevin? I'm confused, Chloe."

"You can see whomever you want, but I'd rather have it be Trent."

Maggie swallowed her coffee. "I'm going to bed. I need to get my beauty rest, so I don't have dark circles and bags under my eyes. I'll be ready by five."

~ * ~

"Have you seen that car before?" Chloe asked as they pulled away from the house before five.

"No. Have you?" Maggie heard apprehension in Chloe's voice.

"Well, the other day the car was there, but just now there was a man sitting in the car. He appeared to be watching the house."

"Don't be silly. Why would someone be watching the house?" Maggie chided her friend.

"You're right. He probably lives in the neighborhood or is a renter."

"If I had to guess, he's a renter, trying to figure out where he's going. I know where we're headed though. Thank you for keeping quiet about me going to the party." Maggie glanced at her friend.

"Trent will be happy to see you there. I know you don't want to hear it, but I know he likes you."

"I know."

"You know what? That he'll be happy to see you or that he likes you?"

"That he'll be happy I'm there. You're going to love the Triple R. It reminds me of home."

Chapter Eight

People dotted the backyard and pool area. They stood in small and large groups, talking and laughing. They sat at the round tables poolside where children giggled, swam and splashed. In the distance were two large canopies. One covered the grills and wide expanse of food offered, while the other had more tables and chairs.

Maggie's stomach churned with apprehension. She hadn't expected anything this elaborate when Trent invited her to the party. She guessed the crowd to be a hundred and fifty plus, consisting of friends and family of the team...and Trent.

In the late afternoon sun, she spotted Chad and touched Chloe to tell her, when she caught sight of Trent walking into the house.

"Chloe," Chad yelled.

"Come on." Chloe pulled her arm.

"Hi," the women hollered in unison.

Chad smiled, jogging over to greet them. After kissing Chloe, he said to Maggie, "You made it. Trent will be glad you decided to come."

"I know. He came to the house to deliver the invitation. I'll leave you two alone. I could use a drink and something to eat," Maggie said and strolled toward the food tent.

"I'm glad you came." Trent snuck up behind her. "Beautiful as always."

Maggie turned. "Thank you," she said pushing her nervous, rolling stomach back. His black Stetson shaded his face, along with those blue eyes, from the sun. Her stomach reacted in this manner not because of the need for food, but because of his affectionate smile.

Trent took her hand, and they strolled through the yard *away* from the house.

"Where are you going?" Maggie asked and glanced around, bewildered. "Or better yet, where are you taking me?" She trusted him, but not herself. Being alone with him wouldn't be a good idea. Her body was too willing to open up to him. He had her believing she could love and be loved again, but she wasn't certain if her heart could survive.

"Don't worry, trust me. What were you thinking about?" He let go of her hand, and his arm slid around her waist.

"I was thinking about home." She peered at Trent and then around the grounds. Her heart hammered against her chest.

"Tell me more about where you grew up." He led her into a small stand of trees and released her to continue walking.

"Although my dad works downtown, my parents live outside of Houston on a sprawling ranch. Picture something along the lines of the home on 'Dallas'. Not quite as substantial, but I think you get it. Horses were at my disposal." She grew quiet as they cleared the trees.

Before her was a beautiful flower garden. Immediately she knew where the bouquet Trent had delivered came from. He had taken the time to cut and care for the flowers himself. Along with the daisies and snapdragons he had cut for her, she recognized the gerbera daisies and salvia. She inhaled the sweet scent surrounding her and softened at the thought that a man such as Trent was behind all of this. Many other flowers surrounded her, and she didn't know what they were, other than beautiful.

"Oh, Trent, this is wonderful." She turned to glance behind her. "Did you plant this yourself?"

"There were some wildflowers growing here, and I wanted to add some plants to remind me of home, my mother, and grandmother. I owe them more than can be put into words." The affection for them warmed his smile and eyes as he stood at the edge of the garden.

"Where are they?" she inquired walking through the garden on the path.

"My grandmother passed away, and Mom remarried. I attempted to talk Mom and Pete into moving here, but they wanted to stay in Colorado. They live near the ranch I was raised on." He stopped talking and asked, "What?"

"When I first came to Rolling Rock Ranch, with the rock, iron and wood, it reminded me of the Rockies rather than southwest Florida." Maggie clasped her hands together to keep from playing with her hair.

"Really?" Trent asked with surprise and pride.

"What did you like most about growing up on a ranch?" She bent to smell an unfamiliar flower.

"The horses and land were my favorite things. The land here is different, but riding Majestic feels like heaven no matter where I am. If you had dressed for riding, we could've taken the horses out." He leaned against a tree at the edge of the flowerbed and gazed at her.

"We couldn't have gone riding. You have guests here."

"I know. Is Blue Bonnet named after your home state flower?"

"Yes. How do you know state flowers?" He amazed her by knowing such a useless piece of trivia. Texans knew their blue bonnets, but someone from Colorado would not have grown up with them everywhere.

"My mother loves flowers and is always talking about the ones she wished she could grow. She wanted some blue bonnets, but I guess she never got around to getting some planted."

"Your mother and grandmother would be proud of your garden." She turned and strolled back on the path toward the woods.

"Where are you going?"

"We should get back to the party. I was in search of a beverage and food earlier."

He took her hand and led her out of the garden in the direction of the house. He stopped and pulled her to a halt where they were surrounded by trees.

"Why did we stop?" She glanced around confused.

"I'm glad you came today. I wanted to do this again." He leaned forward and casually kissed her.

He deepened the kiss as her arms wrapped around his neck, only to break contact at the crunching of twigs.

"I know that flower garden is here somewhere," a woman said in earshot.

Trent cleared his throat. "This way. Showing it to Maggie." Three women approached. "Maggie this is Eve, Bella, and Ginny. Ladies, this is Maggie."

The women eyed Maggie from top to bottom, and Bella gave Maggie a twice over.

"It's nice to meet you all," Maggie said to the group who came across as though they didn't care whether it was nice or not. They gave the impression of being better than her as they spoke condescendingly.

"You look familiar. Have we met before?" Bella asked with overconfidence.

"I don't believe so. Do you work at the hospital?"

"No, but I swear I know you from somewhere." Bella gave another slow appraising glance.

"Enjoy the party ladies." Trent took Maggie's hand. "Great to see you could make it." His pace was rather quick as he steered her back toward the house.

Trent's home had a porch, which wrapped around the entire house and reminded her of where she grew up. In her Texas childhood home, the second story had spectacular views of the ranch.

Maggie followed him through the crowd and into the kitchen where the caterers prepared food. He pulled a glass from the cupboard. "What would you like to drink?"

"Water would be fine."

"I should see to the rest of my guests. Will you be okay?" He handed her a full glass.

"Yes. Would you mind if I took a quick tour of the house?" she asked in hopes of going upstairs and seeing the view.

"Sure," he said and left the room before she could explain her request.

She wondered why Trent seemed to be annoyed and suspected maybe the women had seen them kissing, before making enough noise to be heard.

Bella hadn't appeared pleased to discover Trent and Maggie alone. The snotty tone and the 'I'm better than you' looks she had received from the woman clued her in.

Was there a history between Trent and Bella? From the exchange, she suspected it would've been a falling-out. She also wondered about the comment by Bella, as if she knew Maggie. From what she recollected, the two had never met until today.

Maggie finished her glass of water and headed into the front of the house to the living room and parlor. She wondered if Trent thought of it as a parlor or office. Decorations in browns and tans, with a mix of navy, gave a strong presence a man lived here. Despite not being a fan of brown for interiors, she found the rooms inviting and warm. In the front entry, a staircase led to the second floor.

She climbed the stairs and passed a couple returning to the party. They exchanged cordial smiles. Most of the guests stayed outside around the pool and house. Kids splashed and yelled in the pool, and the 'clink' of horseshoes hitting the poles could be heard.

She wandered the hall and turned into a room with a desk, computer and shelves. This was an office. The corner displayed an antique file cabinet, and it appeared to be old enough to maybe have been his grandfather's.

She crossed the room to the window and sat on the settee. Facing the entrance of the property, fields spread as far as her eyes could see, and horses dotted the landscape, grazing and lazing about. Much like when she first arrived at the ranch to meet Blue...and Trent.

Home.

Maggie had known feelings would come to the surface when she asked if she could give herself the five-cent tour.

Damned Mike! Why did he have to ruin things? Screw him. At least she was alive and had a life of her own. Not one under scrutiny twenty-four seven like his living on a bail bond awaiting a court hearing.

She stood up, wiped her cheeks, and scolded herself, "It's time to move on."

The next room, a guest bathroom and a door from the bathroom led into a guest bedroom. She entered the bedroom through the hall door. It was decorated with hues of blue to coordinate with the bath. The house felt like Trent, masculine colors and lines, yet not what she expected. He had to have had a decorator come in and help pull it all together. Then again, he knew his flowers and maybe had a flare for interior design.

At the other end of the hallway, she knocked on the closed double doors. Another bedroom? This room must have a view of the pool and barn. No answer, she turned the knob and slowly opened a door.

A massive mahogany four-poster bed with aqua and light brown bedding announced this was the master bedroom. He had matching mahogany furniture scattered throughout the room. The walls were done in a dark chocolate brown, with the plaster effect she had seen on one of those redecorating shows. The interesting blend of colors and textures made the room very inviting.

Was she intruding on his privacy? No, he'd said she could take a tour, and the view was what she came for. Maggie stepped to the window and peered out to the guests on the lawn, around the pool and house. Everywhere her eyes roamed there was rolling hills and lush green. She sat on the window seat and enjoyed the view for a moment before she decided to mingle with the other guests.

Outside she grabbed a beer from the tub of ice and beverages. Chloe chatted with some of the people who had been at the party the other night, so Maggie wandered around the pool to the tables situated at one end and sat. She took a long swig. Ice cold, the only way she liked beer.

A few kids did cannon balls into the pool, seeing who could make the biggest splash. She overheard a conversation at a nearby table and, glancing sideways, observed the three women from the flower garden with their heads together.

"You know she's the flavor of the week, Bella. He'll be back," Ginny said to Bella.

"She is *so* far beneath him. He's got money, a great house, and is hot to boot. Bella, you knock his socks off, girl. Don't worry about some floozy. She's temporary," Eve chimed before stuffing a barbecued chicken wing in her mouth.

"If she's so *temporary*," Bella haughtily asked, "why did someone see them at the pre-offshore party together?"

"It's not like you two didn't have a great time. He'll be back. He is a man after all," Ginny replied, reaching over and touching Bella's forearm.

"He's not ready to commit to someone after Janet cheated on him. They stayed together for a long time, so it will take him time," Eve said, striving to make excuses for Trent.

"Janet was with him for his money, and when she found someone with more she cheated on him and then left him," Ginny said.

"A month before the wedding," Eve added quickly. "Surely you can understand why he would be commitment phobic at this point?"

"I would *never* do anything like that to him," Bella commented while tossing her long wavy red hair over her shoulders.

"Well, maybe he thinks you would. You know men talk, and your past relationships weren't the best. I'm sure someone took it upon themselves to tell him all about you. Someone who might be jealous of you," Eve said.

"After Janet, the man needed to be alone. Bella, if you want to be with him make a play for him or quit talking about it," Ginny said, evidently tired of the conversation.

"I remember where I've seen her."

"What are you talking about?" Eve questioned, annoyed the conversation about Trent continued.

"Back in the garden, I asked if we had met before because she looked *so* familiar. I remember where I've seen her... And I *intend* to make sure Trent knows what kind of woman this Maggie is before it goes *any* further between them," Bella said with determination.

Where could Bella possibly know her from, Maggie wondered.

The abrupt action as Maggie stood set the empty glasses and bottles to rattling and drew the attention of the terrible trio. She snatched her beer prior to it toppling and stood a little taller before she stalked off to the barn.

Chapter Nine

Trent talked with the elderly couple who lived on the neighboring ranch about his interest in acquiring their land to add to his current spread. From the porch where they stood, he watched Maggie get up, almost knock the table over, and leave the area in a hurry. Eve, Bella, and Ginny sat one table away from her.

"Excuse me," Trent said, touching the old man's arm. "I see a guest I need to talk to." He left in the direction Maggie had headed.

The pool area cleared and not seeing her anywhere, he slowed his pace and wondered where she'd disappeared.

The barn.

He slipped in and latched the door to keep others from entering.

What did the girls say to send her off? He would have to be casual about his inquiry and not act as though he were an interrogator.

At the far end of the barn he found her with Blue's nose touching her forehead. While she talked to the mare he relaxed and listened to her soft voice.

"People are so cruel, Blue. They don't care who they hurt in the end."

Trent leaned against a pole and continued to listen.

"Horses are the best friends anyone could have. They listen to everything you say, and sometimes you don't have to say anything. I think horses are better than dogs." Silence fell between owner and horse. Trent knocked on a wood post. She and Blue both lifted their heads.

Blue whinnied and backed up a step.

"You startled us."

"I saw you take off and thought I'd check on you." He rubbed Blue's neck. The mare stepped closer to him. "What made you come to the barn?" He hoped it came out in a causal manner.

"I thought it would be a good time to pay her a visit. What's the real story behind why you moved here from Colorado?"

The direct question startled him. The woman was on a mission to find some answers. He intended to spend more time with her, wanting her to be comfortable and open up, so he decided it couldn't hurt to tell the truth. If he showed he trusted her, in return she might tell about her past.

"I had a long-term relationship with a woman, got engaged, the situation took a turn, and we split. I wanted to leave and start fresh someplace else," he said in basic terms.

"What happened?"

He strolled to a vacant stall and sat on a stack of hay bales. Maggie followed and sat next to him, waiting for him to answer.

"I dated Janet for four years. During those years and while engaged, my life changed in ways I never dreamed it would. You already know some of this, but my grandfather died and left me the ranch. At the time, my mother lived on the ranch, too. She had been dating someone in town.

"Anyway, once Grandpa died, Mom decided to move and marry Pete. Janet decided it wasn't good for me to be alone on the ranch, so she moved in. At the same time, she initiated her campaign to get me to sell the ranch. You see, she wanted the money the land would bring and not the life of a rancher's wife."

Trent paused to see if she had an interest in hearing the story. She nodded, and he continued. "Janet started spending the night with her friends a few times a week. I believed her. I found out about a month before we were to be married she'd been sleeping with another man. She planned on leaving me prior to the wedding, but the situation forced us both to reassess our relationship."

"Did you know the person she cheated with?" There was sadness in her tone.

"Yes." He looked down at his boots, not caring to remember or tell about that time in his life. "Someone I had known most of my life. He owned some land down the road from ours. He sold to a land developer, and Janet decided to be with him. He had the money she wanted."

"Surely she loved you." She placed her hand on his thigh. Warmth spread up his leg and to his groin.

"I thought so, but she only loved money and thought if I didn't sell the land we wouldn't have money. I never told her any differently. I'm glad I found out when I did."

She leaned in and kissed him on the cheek. He put his arms around her before she could get back to her side of the hay bale. She stiffened, and he wondered if he should let her go? She relaxed, and he pulled her onto his lap.

Trent lightly kissed her cheek. She wrapped her arms around his neck, their lips caressed, and he gave hers a light nip. She moaned as he took possession of her mouth. Their tongues danced while he fondled her back.

She placed her hands on his shoulders, and he was afraid she might push him away. He placed kisses on her neck and ear. Her tongue ran the curve of his ear lobe, and his manhood awoke instantly. He wanted to fill the hunger he so long desired, but knew he couldn't. Not here. Not now.

He slid one hand around to the front of her dress and rubbed her stomach. Slowly, his hand slid until it cupped her full breast. He kissed her and sighed at the softness of her skin. He didn't want to make love with her for the first time in the barn. He removed his hand.

"Maggie, we, I…"

"I understand—I'm not what you want." She turned away and started to stand.

"Maggie—" He pulled her back into his lap. "I do want you, if you couldn't tell how much—just not here." He held her close and soothed her with a kiss. "Ah, Maggie, when it happens between us, I want it to be right." He gazed at her face.

Her hair had fallen into her eyes. Delicately he brushed it back and exposed the line on the left side of her face. The back of his hand caressed the scar. "How did you get this?"

Maggie ducked her head. She struggled to move, but he held on a little tighter, not ready to let her go.

He wanted her to open up and be honest with him. He *wanted* emotional intimacy with her as well as physical intimacy, and to get there they needed to trust each other. Despite what she might think, they had a relationship. Not clearly defined but a relationship. Trent cleared his throat, cutting the silence.

"Maggie, you can trust me. I'm not going to judge you." He paused. "How did you get it?"

He waited with patience, but couldn't handle the silence when there was no reply. "You cover it well. I want you to know there is no reason to hide *it* or anything else from me. I want you to believe and trust in me. *In us.*"

"What us?" she exclaimed and whipped her head around to glare into his eyes.

"Come on, Maggie. You know there is a connection between us. You feel it as much as I do."

She slid off his lap, stood, and backed away a few steps. "I know we have a good time together, but truth be told, the ink on my divorce papers is barely dry, and I need time to understand what's important to me and *my* life."

"What does that have to do with the scar and how you got it?" he asked, confused and with more force than he intended.

"Everything," she whispered.

Trent barely heard her. She turned to run off, but he stopped her when his hand rested on her shoulder. "Maggie, I'm sorry if I upset you. It wasn't my intent." His heart raced. Raced out of love, out of guilt, out of fear. "I know the scar bothers you, or you wouldn't try to hide it. I understand your need to keep the circumstances to yourself. The scar doesn't affect the way I feel about you." His hand slid from her shoulder and caressed her arm

"It was an accident." Her words dripped with spite, and she pushed past him, storming out the barn door.

He suspected it to be much more than an accident as he stood alone.

He had never seen her this way. He saw her find Chloe and as she spoke made gestures with her arms. He could not, and would not, blame her if she remained mad. He hadn't properly handled his curiosity about her scar.

Trent was about to approach her when a hand clapped him on the shoulder. While the person talked to him, Trent kept her in his sight. Disappointment set in as he watched her get into the BMW. He wanted to continue their conversation from the barn.

~ * ~

Maggie's car turned, entering Rolling Rock Ranch. Balloons floated announcing Trent was having a party today at the ranch.

"Damn it!" Kevin banged his hand on the steering wheel. He pulled to the side of the road out of sight.

After watching and waiting for two hours, his payoff came. Her little convertible squealed pulling onto the main road. She scowled and talked to herself. With her car top down, the radio thumped to the bass and her hair danced behind her while she continued to have a conversation with herself.

They entered the freeway and he trailed behind by one car length between them. She was picking up speed, so he followed her pace. She flexed her hands and screamed, like she was frustrated. A few drivers glanced at her as they passed, and she stopped yelling. The beat of the bass from her radio grew louder.

Why didn't she stay longer? Did something happen? Maybe *now*, things could work to his favor again. Kevin looked forward to taking something of Mike's, after Mike had taken from him. When Mike had botched the deal, Kevin had to make up the difference out of his pocket. He fully intended to get what he wanted now.

He wanted to know more about what happened with Mike and Maggie's marriage. He made himself scarce when everything happened. Not wanting to make inquiries for fear of drawing attention to himself. Would she be easy to manipulate as Mike had been? If so, *she* would be his ticket.

Maybe talk her into drinks, which could lead to dinner and maybe dessert back at his place. He realized the last thought was a little presumptuous. Maggie wasn't like his other girls who skipped right to dessert.

He drove the three and a quarter miles to his place once she made the turn into her driveway. She'd driven fast enough that they'd made it back in under two hours. Once at home, he dialed her number.

"Hello." Maggie breathed heavily over the line.

"Hi Maggie, Kevin. Is this a bad time?" He sat on the soft, buttery leather couch and gazed at the view they shared of the Gulf of Mexico.

"No, just getting ready for bed." Her voice softened.

"I had such a good time at lunch the other day with you, I was hoping maybe we could meet for drinks and dinner." His body responded after seeing her and he adjusted the crotch of his shorts.

"How about tomorrow night?"

He paused for a moment stunned by how quickly she jumped at the invitation. "Where would you like to go? I'll make reservations."

"Seven o'clock at Marina Jack's. You decide which of the restaurants."

"I'll call you if the time changes." Pleased, he put on the charm. "Sweet dreams, Maggie." He leaned back into the leather unzipping his shorts to further the relief of his erection.

"Good night, Kevin." Her line went dead.

He spread his legs taking the thick length in his hand, pleasuring himself with thoughts of Maggie until he moaned and his body shuddered with release.

~ * ~

Upset enough by Trent's actions and words yesterday, she jumped too quickly at Kevin's invitation and now had another date with him. Maggie cursed Trent. But she could only blame herself for her actions. She'd started things with the simple kiss on his cheek and let the situation build in the heat of passion. There was no denying a physical attraction to the man. But she couldn't bring herself to believe they had a relationship beyond friendship.

Later, upon arriving at Marina Jack's, the valet held her car door open, and she slid out, taking the claim check. She smoothed her cotton skirt and ran her fingers through her hair.

Inside, she checked the Deep Six Lounge for Kevin. She spotted him at the bar, talking to a brunette who could've walked off the pages of the latest fashion magazines. Maggie could tell her lips were collagen filled, as they were too large for her mouth and face. And the boobs? They were fake, too. If they were any larger the poor thing would tip over.

The woman stopped chatting with Kevin as Maggie approached. If a copperhead snake could wear lipstick, Maggie was looking at one. Not the jealous type, the venomous snake didn't scare Maggie. The woman could have him if she wanted.

"Hi, Kevin, you got here early." She turned and addressed the woman. "Hi, I'm Maggie, a friend of Kevin's. Care to join us?" Maggie hoped she'd say yes.

"Thank you, but I'm meeting someone here. We were passing time. Have a great dinner." The brunette moved away from them.

"Sorry, I didn't mean to scare her off. She's more than welcome to dine with us."

"No sweat, babe. She's my ex-girlfriend. I was waiting. She came in, so we struck up a conversation."

The *babe* remark sent a bad shiver up her back. He took her elbow and led her away from the bar. "I made a reservation in the Bayside Dining Room."

Ex-girlfriend? If that's an ex, then what could he like about her? Thin lips and normal boobs. Nothing fake on Maggie's body.

The hostess sat them at a table on the upper level with a view more spectacular than the main floor. It overlooked Sarasota Bay and the various-sized boats and yachts docked at the marina. To her, the best thing about Marina Jack's was the view. The sunset from the dining room beat most of the competition as one of the best places to watch the sun go down.

The waiter delivered their drinks, and a server delivered a breadbasket. Maggie took a roll and while spreading on a pat of butter asked, "Being a VP at Franklin are you required to travel a lot?"

"I'm not required but like to when I can. You can't beat free international travel."

"I suppose not. Where have you been?" She took a bite of her roll.

"All over, but I prefer Europe. They know how to have a good time. In a few years, I plan on taking my yacht to the Mediterranean."

"Have you been there before?" Maggie relaxed with the conversation and enjoyed hearing about his travels.

"Only a couple of times. Not long enough to explore the islands or culture." Kevin stopped talking when the waiter approached.

With their orders taken, Kevin took the conversation in a different direction. "What went wrong with your relationship that led to the divorce?"

She took a sip of her wine. "Mike became focused more on money than on our relationship. I wouldn't tolerate it, and Mike took it too far."

"How did he focus on money? He was a pharmacist at the hospital with a regular paycheck." His eyebrows scrunched inward.

She welcomed the interruption from the delivery of her salad. He knew buttons to push that put her on edge. She didn't understand why anytime he mentioned Mike she felt queasy. Yet, if she wanted to find out more she would have to put up with the questions.

"*Illegally*, he focused on money illegally." An edge of impatience crept into her voice. Something, *someone*, caught her eye before she could ask Kevin again about how he knew Mike.

Chad sat at a table, drinking water. She couldn't believe Chloe would've sent him to keep an eye on her.

"Will you excuse me?" Maggie stood. "I need to use the restroom."

She passed Chad and said, "Follow me." In the restroom hall, she asked, "How could you? Did she send you to watch me?"

"Who?"

"Don't give me that. Chloe." Seriously, he didn't know what she was talking about?

"She didn't send me here. I'm meeting a friend. I do live here, you know."

"Sorry." Maggie grimaced in shame. "I remember now that Chloe did mention you had plans. Have a good night."

She left him standing in the hall and, walking back, caught a glimpse of Bella at a table with the other two women from the party. Not wanting to gain their attention, she avoided contact of any kind and continued to the table where Kevin conversed on his cell phone.

She approached, and he stood to help with her chair, continuing his phone discussion while doing so. Then he proceeded to walk away as he held up his index finger. She couldn't believe he left her sitting by herself without a word.

Kevin returned after their meals had arrived. She had waited for him and lost her appetite. Thankful for the bread and salad prior to the main meal, she watched him dig into his meal with zest, as though he hadn't eaten for weeks.

"What's wrong? Don't like your food?" he managed to ask between bites.

"It's cold, and I'm not hungry anyway."

"How did you get this scar?" Kevin slowly ran his finger on her jaw across the scar, too seductive for her taste.

"An accident." She twisted her face from his hand.

"You're still beautiful, babe."

Her jaw clenched at another *babe* reference. "How did you know Mike so well?" She took a sip of wine.

"We did business together."

"I know, but what *kind* of business?" She held firm not to let go of her need for answers.

"I sold drugs. He bought them," Kevin said before adding, "That's the pharmaceutical business."

"Tell me more about your relationship."

"My company does business throughout the States, and Texas is one of them. Mike was one of our contacts, so I frequently worked with him." The bill arrived, and Kevin laid his credit card on the table.

Her gut told her he knew more. To get more information out of him, she would have to reveal the whole truth behind her and Mike. Something she wasn't ready to do—not for Kevin or Trent. He signed the bill and helped her with her chair.

Maggie handed the valet her claim ticket at the main entrance, and Kevin waited with her.

"What about your car?" She noticed he didn't hand a ticket to the valets.

"I'm staying the night on my yacht, which is docked here."

She nodded her head in understanding.

"You want to come see it?" He stepped closer.

"No—thank you."

"Dinner Monday night?"

"Monday won't work." The valet pulled up, and she added, "Kevin, I can't see you anymore."

He pulled her body flush with his. The next thing she knew, his lips found hers.

She pushed him away, and in a quiet, assertive tone said, "*Kevin*, stop. I don't want a relationship with you. Thank you for dinner, but no more. It's too uncomfortable because of Mike." Sliding onto the car seat, she drove away quickly without making a scene.

"God, why is all of this happening to me? All I want is to have a normal life. And why are these men finding the need to kiss me? Ugh—Kevin, of all guys." She couldn't have done much to stop the kiss. Being in public had made it easy for Kevin to steal it.

Chapter Ten

Trent answered the door to find the *last* person he wanted to see or speak to. "Hello, Bella. What can I do for you?"

"May I come in?"

"I'm sorry, no." He stepped onto the porch and closed the door. "I need to go to the barn. We can walk and talk at the same time." A lie but he didn't want to be in the house with her. He didn't trust her.

"Okay." She followed and walked alongside him. "I stopped to thank you for inviting me to the party. I had a wonderful time."

"A phone call would've been fine."

"Well...I also wanted to tell you, your *girlfriend* is seeing another man."

"What are you talking about, Bella?" Annoyed, he picked up the pace.

"I remembered where I had seen her before."

He stopped in his tracks and with a level stare stated, "She has a name, *Bella*—and its Maggie."

"Anyway, I was at Bonefish, and she was there with the same guy I saw her with last night at Marina Jack's, in the Bayside Dining Room."

"And you're telling me this because?" he asked, nonchalant. Maggie was going on dates. His teeth gnashed against each other, his stomach knotted, and his shoulders tensed.

"Trent, I think you should be made aware of her unfaithfulness. I don't want to see you get hurt again." Bella reached out and touched his arm.

He jerked his arm and whole body away.

"Bella, you don't like seeing me happy with another woman other than yourself. I don't need you coming and telling me what guests from my party are doing with *their* lives." He released a little anger and tension out on Bella. It felt good but didn't ease the hurt of Maggie being with someone else.

"So, she's *not* your girlfriend?"

"I never implied whether she was or wasn't." He threw Bella's fishing expedition on to dry land. "But," he stopped, turned to face her and continued, "I can tell you this, *you* are not my girlfriend and won't be again. You only want what I have, money. Now, if you'll excuse me." Trent marched into the barn and went in search of Juan. He knew he should never have dated the daughter of a family friend. It only made severing the relationship that much harder.

Instead of finding Juan, Chad approached him. "Hey boss. I was looking for you."

"What's up?" he asked short, preoccupied by his conversation with Bella.

"You in a hurry?"

"No, what's up?" He stopped walking and paid attention to Chad.

"I was out last night at Marina Jack's and—"

"Let me guess, you saw Maggie?"

"How did you know?" Chad asked perplexed.

"Bella gave me an ear full, but the one thing she didn't say was *who* Maggie was with."

"Kevin Shaw."

"What?" Trent's blood boiled like a teapot ready to blow its lid.

"Yeah, I was surprised too."

"Thanks." He turned abruptly, exited the barn and headed back to the house.

He dialed Maggie's number and paced the wood floor of the office. He wanted the chance to talk her out of anything further between her and Kevin. Unsure of what to say, he at least wanted her to be aware he knew about her dates with Kevin. From there he didn't have a plan.

"Kevin, of all people." The guy was bad news when it came to women. And why Maggie? She's far from the type Kevin usually goes for. Trent wanted to find out what was going on.

Maggie answered with a casual hello.

"Maggie, hi, it's Trent." He continued pacing.

"Hi." She paused a moment. "The party was very nice."

"Thank you." He let their intimate moment in the barn go after learning about Kevin and needed to stay focused on his reason for calling.

"Chloe tells me you have another race this weekend. When do you leave?"

"I hear you've been on some dates." He had jumped right to the point and was met by silence.

"Chad," she sighed.

"Yes, Chad. You can go out with Kevin, but I want to know why?" He didn't want to sound jealous but rather concerned.

"Excuse me?" She spit out the words with disdain. "I don't believe I asked *you* whether or not I could go on a date. I am perfectly capable of making my own decisions, and for the future, I hope you remember that." She paused, quick to add, "And another thing...*don't* think you can call here and issue orders to me as if I'm some puppet. Is my date the only reason you called?"

"No." Hearing a dial tone Trent threw the phone on the desk. Was he wasting time on Maggie? No. He didn't know if it was her scar, or unknown past, that captivated him, gave him reasons to continue his pursuit. He couldn't deny the sexual attraction between them, which fueled the fire more.

~ * ~

Refreshed from sleeping, Maggie rolled over and peered at the note she'd found on her bedroom railing after her night shift. 'Trent called. Call when you get home. Said he was sorry?' She picked up the phone and dialed the number.

"He should be sorry." She rested against the pillows and pulled up the covers. "Questioning me about Kevin." She listened to his line ring.

"Good morning, Maggie. I'm glad you called."

"I didn't think you'd appreciate a call after midnight, so I waited to call back."

"I want to apologize for my phone call yesterday. You're right. It's none of my business, and I'll stay out of it. I'm sorry for pushing you about your scar when we were in the barn. I didn't mean to, but I do want you to know you can talk to me about it."

"Thanks. Apology accepted." The sun shining through the sheers of the closed patio door seemed a little brighter.

"I know you need some time. I went through something similar after Janet."

"I don't think what happened with you and Janet is *anything* like what happened between Mike and me." She threw back the covers, hopped out of bed, and approached the patio doors.

"Why don't you tell me about it, and we can compare the two situations."

"Let's say I don't trust easily these days." Annoyed, she pulled back the sheer and opened the door. "My view about money in my life has changed since Mike. If you don't mind, I don't care to ruin my day talking about this." She paused, stepped onto the deck and took a relaxing breath. The water had a calming effect, and Maggie closed her eyes. "I'm sorry for hanging up on you."

"You had every right to get upset with me. I behaved like an idiot." Met by silence, he continued, "Can I take you to lunch today? A truce of sorts."

"No," she said bluntly and opened her eyes.

"Oh." Success. She had made him feel guilty if only for a minute.

"I wouldn't say you behaved like an idiot either. I could meet you tomorrow."

"Are you planning on coming for a ride on Blue tomorrow?"

"I have to work. What are you thinking?"

"Cooking on the grill, but if that doesn't work—"

"It will work if you can have me fed and on my way by one." She walked back into the room and sat on the small sofa.

"Can do, little lady," he said in his best John Wayne voice. "I'll feed you with time to spare. See you tomorrow and have a good night at work."

"I will. Thanks."

She went downstairs and found Chloe on the deck, reading.

"Did you call Trent?" Chloe asked when Maggie stepped outside.

"Yes. Hey, why don't you go with me? I'm going riding and then staying for lunch tomorrow." Maggie sat down in the chaise next to Chloe.

"Thanks, but I made plans. So, how was your date with Kevin?"

"Not great. He was on his phone for a good duration of the time. I waited for him to return to the table and when he did return, my food was cold so I didn't eat. The worst part was after dinner when he kissed me at the valet." Just mentioning it gave her shivers.

"What?" Chloe exclaimed and sat upright.

"It was before I got into my car. It was awful. I couldn't do anything about it. I told him I wasn't interested and left." She rubbed her arms to make the chill go away.

"How did he take that?"

"I think he'll need to be told again before it sinks into his thick skull. I have the feeling he's used to getting what he wants and didn't like my telling him no."

"I hope you don't mind, I've decided to go with Chad and the team to their next race at Dania Beach."

"I'm glad you're having a good time." Maggie stood. "I'm going in. I need to get some coffee and something to eat."

"What is Trent sorry about?" Chloe followed her into the kitchen.

"He asked about my scar at the party, which upset me, as you know. Then he called, asking me about seeing Kevin, and I hung up on him." It wasn't the full truth but close enough. She didn't want to open up about the sexual closeness in the barn.

"You hung up on him?"

Maggie sat at the counter with her bowl of cereal and coffee. "Trent is not my boyfriend and can't tell me who I can and can't see. As it turns out, I won't be seeing Kevin again but am going to have lunch with Trent tomorrow before work."

"Who kisses better? Trent or Kevin?"

Maggie pulled the spoon out from her mouth, raised her eyebrow, came eye-to-eye with Chloe, and crunched on her granola.

"Well, who's better?"

She swallowed and took a sip of coffee. "Do I really need to answer that?"

"Maybe I should ask for more detail about Trent's kisses."

"You know enough, and unless you want to divulge information about Chad, I'd drop the subject."

"Okay, I'll let you finish eating in peace. I'm glad to hear you won't be seeing any more of Kevin."

Chloe returned to the deck, and Maggie finished her breakfast. Her brief conversation with Chloe had her daydreaming about Trent.

As upset as she had been in the barn when he stopped kissing and caressing her, she was thankful. He had been right about nothing happening between them in the barn. Maybe the sexual tension between them was to blame for her anger when she left.

Then there was the issue of her body and its reaction to his touch. He had her swimming in a pool of mixed emotions. Not to mention, warm body fluids.

~ * ~

"Hey, beautiful," Trent yelled to her, as she walked from the barn after her ride.

"Am I too early?"

"Nope. What can I get you to drink?"

"Water would be great."

He went inside and came back with a large tray loaded with plates, silverware, burgers and drinks. "Did you have a nice ride?" He placed the meat on the hot grill.

"Yes. I know I've said this before, but you have such a gorgeous place here, Trent. The riding paths are well maintained, cleared of low branches and other obstacles."

"I need to go get the rest of our lunch. I'll be right back."

She watched him disappear into the house and then browsed the grounds. He and his ranch hands did a great job of keeping things in tiptop shape.

"I hope this is good. I'm not too bad of a cook, but never claimed to be a chef," he said, approaching the patio. Without wasting time, he jumped right to the subject closest to his heart. "Am I wasting my time, Maggie? Because if there's someone else, I don't want to interfere." He flipped the burgers, trying to be casual but anxiously awaited her answer.

"I met with Kevin to get more information about Mike. I wanted to know if Kevin knew anything about Mike's drug dealings." Shit! It slipped out. Here came the questions.

"Drugs?" A troubled expression crossed Trent's face.

"I've said enough. I told Kevin I'm not interested and don't want to see him again." She paused a moment. "*God*, why am I explaining myself to you?"

"Maggie," he said, hushed.

Silence fell between them. She spread some barbeque sauce on her bun, then piled on a piece of lettuce, a slice of tomato, a slice of cheese, and some bacon.

"When do you leave for Dania Beach?" She was glad he didn't press further about Mike and the drugs.

"Tomorrow morning. Your burger," he said, and she held out her plate with the bun open.

They ate their lunch, keeping the conversation on horses while Trent talked about the business side of the ranch. Finished eating, he insisted on taking care of the clean up then walked Maggie to her car.

"Thank you for lunch. I had a nice time. Good luck on the race," she said as they neared her car.

"The pleasure was all mine." He stepped closer, crowding her a little.

She backed up against her car door. "Well, I guess I'll talk to you soon." Her voice trembled as he eased closer.

He effortlessly pulled her into his arms and delivered a kiss. Unable to help herself, she increased the intensity with her lips as he held her closer. Maggie broke the seal between them. He opened her car door. She slid behind the steering wheel and drove away as if nothing had happened. Only something *had* happened between them.

~ * ~

Kevin sat in his Escalade on the right side of the road, pulled out of the way from traffic and slightly away from the ranch. He handled a few business calls while watching and when he observed her car leaving the ranch, he sat straighter.

He had followed Maggie from her house earlier, not pleased to see she stayed at Trent's so long. You do not ride a horse for nearly four hours. Something *more* was going on.

The other night she pushed him away and said she didn't want to see him anymore. He had tasted the sweetness he *so* long desired. The kiss had been a bold move to make with her but they had several dates. Yet, it cost him. His timing had been off.

He would monitor her closely, with the need to know if she were involved with Trent on a personal level. Watching more closely than before.

Kevin followed her to the hospital before going to the office where he made a call. After giving his narc Ryan a briefing of the situation, he said, "I need you to watch her twenty-four seven and notify me of *anything* involving Trent Randall." Kevin paced in front of his corner office windows. "I followed her to the hospital, so you don't need to start watch again until eleven tonight." Pausing for a moment, he asked, "Any questions?"

"No sir."

"Let me know if something happens with Randall, *immediately*." Kevin hung up and thought about how he was going to get everything he wanted from Maggie. Getting back at Mike no longer matter to him. This was all about Maggie.

~ * ~

Around nine Thursday morning, Maggie woke and went downstairs. She found a note from Chloe she had missed when she got home. 'Stayed with Chad and leaving in the morning. Be back late sometime Monday night. Call if you need me.' She flipped the switch on the coffee pot. The phone blinked, signaling voice mail.

The first one, from her mother, asked the standard question about how she was doing. Upon hearing the second message, she stood in shock. *Kevin?* He'd called to apologize and wanted to make it up to her by taking her to dinner. Goosebumps crept up the back of her spine, and she shivered.

She poured a cup of coffee, then walked outside to sit on the deck when the doorbell rang. She peered through the peephole and couldn't believe it—another flower delivery.

Cordial as she opened the door to accept the flowers, she set them on the kitchen counter where she opened the card. 'Please accept my apologies. Kevin'

The arrangement rested in a tall, striped vase filled with orange, yellow and red gerbera daisies. Beautiful and stunning, yes, but accept his apology, *no way*. Although she had no solid proof, she was certain Kevin knew Mike other than as a business contact, and his *babe* remarks were inappropriate.

With the three flower bouquets from Kevin, Trent's, and the one from Chad, the house bloomed with floral scents and created the feel of being in a florist shop. Maggie would not give into Kevin and his flowers, no matter *how* gorgeous the arrangements.

She couldn't throw them away. She wanted to, but couldn't. The flowers were beautiful, and she knew someone had taken the time to prepare the display.

Instead of setting them where she would see them, she carried them into the guest bathroom and situated them on the countertop.

"Perfect. It brightens up the room a bit, and I won't have to see them, or think about *him*." She went onto the deck where she relaxed for the rest of the morning before going into work.

Her mind wandered to Trent and the race at Dania Beach. Dania Beach wasn't that far of a drive.

Chapter Eleven

Sunday morning Trent wished Maggie rather than Chloe had traveled with him and the team. Chad and Chloe had grown close during such a short time frame, making it hard for him and his feelings for Maggie. He wanted the same closeness with Maggie.

He reminded himself Chad and Chloe had known each other prior to now. Something he didn't have with Maggie. He dragged his sorry ass out of bed and geared up for race day.

The temperamental Atlantic Ocean waters would prove to be challenging for the best of the experienced racers. Spectators crowded the beach, but there was enough room for kids to run around and build sand castles.

Trent approached the staging area and picked up his pace the moment he laid his sights on her. Maggie had taken time from work to be there.

She turned to him as he approached the group. "You made it," he said and embraced her. "I thought you had to work."

"I made a few changes. I hoped to surprise you." Her eyes sparkled with happiness, and he let the warmth from them spread throughout his body.

"Do I get a good luck kiss?" Without hesitation, her lips came to life on his and stayed planted until he reluctantly broke away. "That should bring more than good luck. We should win the checkered flag for sure."

"I hope so. Now go get it."

Trent gave her another quick kiss. He joined Lance and Alan in the boat. The three-man crew checked their headsets to make sure they could communicate clearly with each other and tested them with the crew on land.

Trent brought the engine to life. The steering wheel vibrated under his hands. He smiled as the trembling spread throughout his body. He drove the boat into the milling area and tried to clear his head of any thoughts about Maggie and that kiss. His focus needed to be on the race and the waters ahead.

"This guy's gonna drop the green flag fast," Alan said while in the parade lap.

"Yeah," Trent said into his helmet mic. "You guys ready?" The ocean had the boat undulating, and they worked to keep it in line.

"Yeah, man," both Lance and Alan replied.

"Drop your helmet, Lance," Trent said. "Let's do this."

"Yellow...Yellow...Yellow...Yellow...Yellow..." Alan instructed. "Go, go, go, go, go, go, go," he yelled as the green went up.

"Where's the buoy?"

"Right there," Alan answered Trent, and shouted to Lance, "Go, go!"

"All right, here we go." Trent took the turn. The high waves and the rough wakes made it difficult to see the other boats.

"To the left a little bit. Right there. To the left, to the left... Right there." Looking around, Alan said, "We're on course now. To the left, to the left. Right there."

"They're going on the inside of us?" Trent asked as they bounced around the boat.

"No, we're good, baby. He's a hundred yards on our left side. You're right on the edge there, big guy," Alan answered.

"I see it."

"You see it?"

"Yeah, I see it. Where is the other boat?" They bobbed on the seat, and Trent made an effort to glance to the sides and then behind them. He couldn't see much and focused on the open water in front.

"He's twenty yards on the outside, riding with us." Alan said, twisting and turning in his seat.

"All clear. He's on our five o'clock," Alan said to Trent on lap four, turn three. "Go ahead. Go ahead. Go ahead." The boat continued to bounce on the water.

"Shit!" Trent yelled and held on tight to the wheel as he lost control of the boat.

Clipped in the back, left corner by another boat, Team Seahorse spun and rolled, bouncing on the water several times before coming to a stop...upside down.

"Oh, my God, Trent!" Maggie screamed at the horror happening in front of her.

They were wearing life vests, but were caught below the flipped boat. Alan came to the surface and waved both of his arms overhead. Within a matter of seconds, the medical helicopter hovered over the boat and deployed the rescue divers. The patrol vessels screamed across the water to the scene, and Lance came to the surface with Trent. A yellow flag waved in the air to notify the other racers to slow down and use caution.

The divers positioned Trent, unconscious, onto the backboard, removed his helmet, and cleared his airway. He coughed, and one of the divers turned his head as he threw up the salt water he had inhaled. They secured the straps and cautiously lifted the backboard onto the rescue boat. Lance and Alan, shook up but fine, kept an eye on the first rescue boat as it left with Trent.

"I need to go to him, Chloe," Maggie said. "Chad, can you get me in the ambulance?"

"I don't know. You're the nurse. Finagle your way in."

"Get me to him. Now," she exclaimed, nervous about the condition Trent could be in.

"Okay," Chad said and rushed her to the medical site. "She's with the team and is a nurse," he told security.

They let them through, and Chad escorted her to the ambulance.

"This is Maggie Carlisle. She's a nurse," Chad stated.

"I'm Trent's wife," she quickly added. "I need to be with him," she whispered at the confusion on Chad's face.

"Okay, but stay out of our way, and let us do our job," one of the EMTs stated.

"Don't worry. I will." She waited with Chad by her side. When they got a moment alone she glanced at Chad and said, "Don't tell anyone what I said unless it's necessary. I only said it so they would let me go with. *Girlfriend* wouldn't cut it."

The EMTs waited for the rescue boat to arrive at shore. Sirens shrieked, and Maggie wanted to cry as they left for the hospital. They placed an oxygen mask on Trent's face and inserted an IV into his arm to give the necessary fluids his body needed.

The EMT continued to monitor his blood pressure and pulse. Vitals were good, but Trent wasn't fully aware.

"I'm right here, Trent." She spoke softly in his ear. "I'm with you. You're okay." She struggled with the tears building up, but gave into the fight and let them fall. Her head fell to his chest, which slowly rose up and down, allowing her to relax.

"Maggie," Trent murmured as the ambulance approached the hospital.

She lifted her head to see his eyes open then close.

~ * ~

He got the call from his informant and the blood boiled in Kevin's veins. He jumped in his Jaguar and headed toward Dania Beach. He knew exactly where to go and he didn't like the fact Maggie took time off work for Trent.

From a distance, he viewed Maggie and Trent exchanging a passionate kiss and his jaw and fists clenched tightly. He witnessed the accident hoping it would be serious enough, permanently erasing Trent from the picture. Unfortunately, it didn't, because she rode off in the ambulance with Trent to the hospital.

He left to return home knowing nothing more would be happening. He headed west on Interstate 75 and called Ryan. "I want you to watch her house and let me know when she gets home." Anger coursed throughout his entire body.

"Okay. Do you want to me to stay after calling you?"

"Yes." You numbskull, he thought. "I need to know what she's doing, more so, where she's going and with who. Notify me if she goes out to Randall's place. I'm aware she has work and friends so don't bother calling me unless Randall is directly involved. Do you understand?"

"Yes boss."

Kevin hung up and slowed the car down. He was going a hundred and twenty and dropped the speed to seventy-five. His rage had him putting more pressure on the gas pedal than he cared for. He knew where and who she was with, so no need to rush.

He didn't care about Mike. In the long run, Mike never screwed him over and he was still in business. Mike was the past. Why bother using Maggie to get back at Mike when he could have her for himself. Trent and Mike had become obstacles and he didn't like it.

Maggie met his womanly criteria—tall, long hair, curvaceous, well-toned and tanned. He also knew she would appreciate the lifestyle he lived, as she came from a wealthy family. He could give her everything her heart desired, if she would only let him in.

~ * ~

When he woke two hours later, Trent found Lance sitting off to the side of his bed. "What happened?"

"We were clipped, and they said you hit your head hard enough that here we are. The only thing I know is we were hit, rolled and ended upside down. How do you feel?"

"What do you think? Like *shit*." There were wires attached to him, and he asked, "When do we get to leave?" His head felt like it had been hit repeatedly with a hammer.

"I don't think we're going anywhere too soon. So, lay back and enjoy the ride, buddy."

"This is one *ride* I don't want to be on." He maneuvered with attached wires into a sitting position. "Is Maggie here?" He swore he had heard her voice earlier.

"Yeah, she rode with you in the ambulance."

"Where is she?" His heart rate monitor picked up on the

quickening beat.

"She's talking to the nurses and doctor. Do you want me to get her?" Lance stood to leave.

"No, but find out how long I have to stay in this place," he said with his voice raised. He didn't want to stay and rest at a hospital. He would rather do it in his *own* bed.

First the nurse and then the doctor came into his room. "You're a lucky man to have a wife who's a nurse. Unfortunately, it doesn't get you discharged any earlier." The doctor flashed a pen light at Trent's eyes and moved it from side to side. "We'll be releasing you tomorrow afternoon." He scribbled notes in a file.

Trent realized the doctor was referring to Maggie with the wife comment.

"We're running some blood work now, and later you'll have a CT scan. You'll be staying through the night for observation due to the head trauma. I'm sure Maggie will take good care of you."

The doctor walked into the hall, and Trent exclaimed, "God damn it, I feel fine." He didn't but wanted to leave the confines of the hospital.

"Relax, man," Lance said as he entered the room. "You can't leave. So knock it off."

"I'd like to see my wife." He smiled at the mere thought.

"Your wife?"

"Yes, can you get Maggie in here?"

"O—kay," Lance said and backed out the door, obviously confused.

"Hey, how's the boat?" Trent inquired before he disappeared.

"Rough shape, but I think we'll have it ready in time for North Carolina."

"Let me know what you need to get it ready and back on the water."

"Will do. Listen, I've got to get back to the hotel to take care of things. Do you want visitors, other than your *wife*?" Lance shook his head with bewilderment on his face.

"If they want to visit me, I have nothing better to do than lie around and chit chat."

"That's a better attitude to have than cursing about it."

"Screw you," Trent said as Lance left. "And find my wife for me," he yelled.

"Trent..." Maggie knocked on the semi-closed door. "Don't be mad at me." She stepped into the room.

"I'm not mad. Come here, and give your husband a kiss," he said, grinning.

"Trent." She positioned her hands on her hips and cocked her head to the side.

"You can call me honey, or any other affectionate name you'd like, dear." The smile got broader as he spoke.

She strolled to the side of the bed, leaned over and planted a dispassionate kiss on his forehead. "That's all you get for now. I don't want to set off any alarms at the nurses' station."

"You're no fun. I would think my wife would want to give her husband a kiss. Something more intimate." She made his pain disappear, being there for him.

"Trent, I had to be with you. The only way they would let me ride in the ambulance was if I was your wife or next of kin."

"So you do have feelings for me? I knew it." He reached out to take her hand in his.

"Don't read too much into this." She sat down in the chair.

"When do you have to leave?"

"I need to go back tonight to work tomorrow morning. I know you'll be in good hands here and on the ride home."

"You mean my wife, who's a nurse, can't get me out of here any earlier?" he asked with his best sad puppy dog face.

"Sorry, my role as wife stops here." She stood up. "You have to listen to the doctor and nurses until tomorrow."

"You're leaving now?"

"It's late. I need to hit the road to be home in time for a good night's sleep."

Maggie bent over and caringly touched her lips to his. Trent took the moment to deepen the kiss, and she didn't resist, pleasing him. He let her go when she pulled away.

"Call me Monday night after seven. I should be home by then."

"I will, dear," he said with a chuckle and wink.

~ * ~

The team hit the road the following afternoon after the hospital released Trent. He couldn't drive per doctor's orders so he thought about Maggie. She took the time off work to watch him race and then she was by his side at the hospital. She cared for him more than she was willing to admit.

He remembered their conversation regarding Kevin and her ex-husband. She didn't go into details, but he wondered about the drugs. How much was Maggie involved? Did she have a history of using or did her ex? And how did Kevin come into play with it all? There were too many unanswered questions.

His thoughts were interrupted when he overheard Chloe talking about returning to Texas.

"You leave tomorrow?" Trent inquired, leaning forward against the front seat of the truck.

"My flight leaves after three." She faced him in a somber mood. "Maggie and I haven't made plans yet on what time we should leave for the airport."

"Maybe, after she drops you off, I can get her to the ranch to go riding and stay for dinner."

A smile formed on Chloe's face.

The drive home went a lot quicker than the drive to Dania Beach, which made him happy. He didn't like being a passenger, and it would feel good to sleep in his own bed. Once the team pulled into the drive, they told him to go into the house and relax.

Trent took hold of his bags to go upstairs, but Blanca, the housekeeper, said, "I take those," and managed to wrestle the bag from his hand. "You go relax on patio." Lance had told her what happened.

"Blanca, you don't need to do that."

"You go relax. I take care of it."

"Gracias." Trent went and sat poolside.

He gazed at the smooth surface of the pool water, reflecting on the race, and wondered if Maggie wasn't to blame in part for the accident. She had him thinking about her at the wrong times.

He shook his head.

It wasn't her fault, but his. He thought about her when his mind should've stayed focused and aware of his surroundings.

If he truly wanted a wife to share his life, he would have to take risks, and Maggie was worth it. Boating had its own dangers, as evidenced by what happened this past weekend.

He would not let racing get in the way of his relationship with Maggie or her get in the way of his racing. She'd already proved she wanted to share in the racing part of his life by showing up at Dania Beach.

Once again, he pondered Kevin and the job he had at the pharmaceutical company. Could Kevin be connected to Maggie's ex-husband?

Chapter Twelve

Tuesday morning arrived with cloudy skies and rain. Maggie walked to the deck doors and watched the waters of the Gulf. What was Trent doing? Was he thinking about her? She wished she could truly savor the great feelings she had when with him, but her past always rushed back when her scar became part of the conversation.

She had failed at her marriage. While Mike was to blame for many things, she also blamed herself. She'd expected they'd be like any newlywed couple and have their struggles for the first few years until established in their careers.

Mike knew how she'd been raised, decided money would make her happy and their marriage work. How could she have been married to someone, occupy the same house, share the same bed, and not realize how little they actually communicated with one another? Maggie speculated, if they had talked more, would things have turned out any different?

She turned away from the window. Her parents were there for her after the accident and, as she reflected on the past, missed their support. Picking up the phone, she called home.

"Mom?" When her mother answered the phone, Maggie broke into tears.

"Maggie? Honey, what's wrong?" Caroline asked.

"Nothing... Everything... I think I'm a little homesick," she answered and wiped her wet cheeks. "Hearing your voice is already making me feel better." She sat on the sofa, the phone cuddled close to her cheek.

"Did something happen? It's not like you to cry for nothing."

"No, not really. I met someone and feel as if I shouldn't be in a relationship. Then today I awoke to a gray, rainy morning, Chloe's leaving, and well, I needed to hear your voice."

"You met someone? How wonderful. What's his name?" She had caught the *met someone* remark.

"Trent. He owns the ranch where Blue is boarded. So many things about it remind me of home. I already missed you and Daddy, and it's only intensified when I'm at the ranch."

"Honey, things are going to happen that will remind you of the past. Unfortunately, not all memories can be good ones. I think you're doing wonderfully, and I'm so proud of you. You've made some big positive life changes. It takes a while to adjust. Give yourself a break, and take some time for yourself. Go get a pedicure or facial. Do something nice for yourself."

If only a pedicure would cure everything ailing her.

"Thanks, Mom. Maybe a shopping spree is in order. Love you. And give my love to Daddy." Maggie hung up and thought life would be so much simpler if the world was how her mother saw it.

~ * ~

Chloe set her bags in the front hall, and tears welled up as Maggie stated, "I wish you didn't have to leave."

"I wish I didn't either. For a few reasons, I would rather be here than in Texas. I'm going to miss you and Chad, but I also have to go back to work. It seems like I've been gone for a long time," Chloe said and sat on the steps. "I realize you know Chad and I played matchmaker. We think you and Trent would be perfect together. You're not going to see Kevin again, are you?"

"*No.* I told you he makes me uncomfortable. I think there's more to what he's told me about his work relationship with Mike. I have to be honest with you...I do have feelings for Trent."

"I think he feels the same way. Let's go, we don't want to miss my plane." Chloe stood and slipped on her sandals.

~ * ~

Trent stood on his bedroom balcony, the expanse of green grass and trees a calm retreat, bringing him inner peace. He loved this land, more than his family's land. He missed some things about Colorado, but he had never felt at home like he did here. This was *his* land, *his* home.

Not able to do anything back in Colorado without the whole town knowing his business, he'd needed to get away from the people who had made his life miserable. He liked that here he was just 'the guy over at the Triple R' to folks.

Trent glanced at his watch and, turning back into the house, took a quick shower and got dressed. The thought of spending time with Maggie today made his stomach quiver with anticipation, not surprising him.

Maggie approached the house with the radio thumping and continued toward the barns. Trent caught her before she got past the house. "Park up here," he said when she stopped the car and turned the radio down.

He wanted to have a serious relationship with Maggie and would treat her as a woman should be treated—with respect. She was more than a boarder at the ranch.

"You are a sight for sore eyes." His heart raced with excitement. He took her hands in his and kissed her, delighted by her acceptance.

"How are you feeling?" she asked with concern in her voice and eyes.

"I'm not playing twenty questions about me *or* the accident. I'm fine and alive. Let's get you riding while I prepare our meal."

"Trent, talk to me about the accident."

"There's not much to say. You saw it. Someone clipped the back of the boat. I smacked my head hard enough to go unconscious. Lance got my belt off and got me to the surface as the divers arrived." Approaching Blue Bonnet's stall, he said, "Hey Blue, guess who decided to come pay a little attention to you."

"No fair," she exclaimed and gave him a playful slap on his arm.

"Okay, so when was the last time you went riding?" Subject

diverted. Right now, he only wanted to talk to the team about what happened.

"I came while you were away. We had a nice long ride, and I cleaned her up myself," she replied as she pulled out blankets from the locker.

"You win." He pulled her into an embrace. "Why don't you take a nice leisurely ride and come back for a great dinner?"

He took possession of her mouth, then released her from the embrace, allowing her to put the saddle on Blue. He checked his watch. "Why don't you return around five?"

"You're not riding?"

"Can't. Doc's orders."

"I'm sorry you won't be joining us, but glad you're playing by the rules. See you then."

Maggie rode off, and he shook his head. "What a woman. Nice backside, too."

"Better move on it then."

Trent turned to find Chad standing behind him, grinning like a fool. "Where'd you come from?" he asked as he walked toward the house.

"Boat barn. Listen, boss, if you're interested, you'd best make it known."

"What are you talking about?"

"I talked to Chloe—"

"Of course you did." He stopped and turned to face Chad.

"I talked to Chloe before she left, and Maggie's gotten flowers from Kevin. Several times."

"I know she's been with Kevin, and we've talked about it. What about these flowers?"

"Maggie's received at least two bouquets Chloe knows of, but when Chloe got back from Dania Beach a new arrangement sat on the counter in the guest bathroom."

Trent's jaw tightened. He clenched and unclenched with every second that passed as Chad talked about the flowers. He was upset with Kevin.

"Thanks." He marched toward the house but turned around to ask, "How's the boat looking?"

"Lance has a guy coming to check it out. He says he's good and can get us ready for North Carolina. How are you feeling?"

"Stiff neck and now a headache. Nothing a little medication can't cure. Which is *why* I'm not riding with Maggie. I have dinner to prepare."

Trent left Chad to continue working and picked up his pace. In the kitchen, slamming drawers and cupboards, Trent cursed Kevin as he worked. "I warned her about him."

Chapter Thirteen

After an exhilarating ride, Maggie returned Blue to her stall. Her emotions had been mixed-up throughout the day, which forced her to sit on a hay bale and take stock of her life. Flashes of home sunk in, and a release of tears spilled down her cheeks.

She needed to get herself together before dinner and sighed with thoughts of Trent. The connection wasn't the same with Kevin as with Trent. What had she been thinking, spending time with Kevin and accepting his flowers. Today her head got screwed back on straight.

Tears wiped away, she wished for a mirror to check her appearance before returning to the house. The screen door slammed a sign Trent was outside and would be waiting for her.

In the bright sunlight, she shielded her eyes with her hand to catch a glimpse of him. Unable to spot him, she headed for the house to freshen up a little before dinner and hide any possible evidence of having cried.

Trent's footsteps came from around the side of the house. She caught her foot on an Adirondack chair. "Damn," she exclaimed and fell to her knees.

"Maggie? Are you okay?" He gently rubbed her arms before helping her up.

"Yes. I'm fine." She put her head down.

"You don't *look* fine." With his finger, he lifted her head by the chin. "You've been crying. Do you want to talk about it?"

"It was a little fall." He stared into her eyes and held onto her arms.

"Really, I'm fine." She turned to go into the house. "I need to use the powder room."

Refreshed, Maggie joined Trent on the patio where he worked at the grill.

"How do you like your steak?" he asked, pointing his tongs toward the grill.

"Medium."

"Coming right up."

"I want to explain about before."

"Okay."

"I had a great time today."

"But?" he prodded with her pause.

"It hit me harder today than in the last few weeks. After my ride," she hung her head at the thought, "your ranch reminds me so much of home."

"You miss Texas."

"I didn't realize how homesick I truly am. I think it helped having Chloe here for a while. I keep busy with work, and now it sort of caught up with me. I'm sorry."

"You have nothing to be sorry about. I'm glad you feel at home here."

Trent came around the grill to her side. She took hold of him around his waist in an unromantic hug. They connected on a more personal and caring level. Before she stepped away from the embrace, she closed her eyes and inhaled the scent of soap.

"Have you talked to your parents?" He went back to the grill.

"My mother practically calls on a daily basis, but my dad is busy with work so I don't get the chance to talk as often to him." She hung her head. "I miss him."

"Your dad?"

"I talked to him a lot back home. You know, Daddy's little girl. I have him wrapped around my finger." She held up her pinky.

"I never would have guessed."

"What's that supposed to mean?" She hadn't meant for it to come out as snidely as it had.

"Your father loves you very much, or he wouldn't have taken the time to get your horse to Florida for you. That's love for a child. Not someone wrapping them around their finger."

Maggie remained quiet, as he seemed to understand the situation. Trent placed their steaks on the plates she held out for him.

They ate dinner on the porch. There was a slight breeze to combat the humidity in the Florida air. Their dinner music was courtesy of the horses' whinnies and hoof stomps and, most of all, the birds singing in the trees.

Content to be silent, she pushed her food around her plate, not eating much. She wanted Trent in a way she never wanted another man before. It had been so long since she had been with a man other than her husband; she was unsure how to go about making the first move.

Trent stood, and Maggie picked up her dishes to follow him, figuring they would end up in the kitchen. She strolled behind and thought about how to corner him and let him know exactly what she wanted.

Back outside she gathered the remainder of the dishes on the table and took them inside. As she set them on the counter, he pulled her hair to the side and placed warm kisses on her neck. Anticipation pumped through her veins like a freight train. Not being able to stand it a minute more, she turned and ran her hands over his chest.

Her breathing and pulse accelerated as he kissed her, while his hands skimmed over her arms and back. Tentative at first, she intensified the kiss, running her tongue across his bottom lip and gave it a light nip. He took possession of her mouth.

Wildfire ran through her body, uncontrollable and spreading to her core lightning fast. With an urgency to satisfy her desires, Maggie slid her hands around the waistband of Trent's jeans until she reached the zipper where she pulled the tab.

He clutched her hands. "What's the hurry?" His hands glided up her arms, onto her chest, crossing her breasts, running his thumbs across her nipples.

She could see the desire building in his gaze as they watched each other. His hands wandered to her hips, lifting her onto the counter. Eye-to-eye, he kissed her lightly at first before increasing the pressure.

Once again, she attempted to divest him of his pants, the fly of his jeans had *somehow* come undone on its own. Undoing the buttons of his shirt, without tearing it off him like she wanted, she spread his shirt open. Her hands ran across his flesh and through his chest hair. She seized hair in between her fingers and gave a gentle tug before fanning them out to enjoy his large ripped frame. She wanted to kiss every inch of him.

He pushed her hands away again and held them secure next to her thighs on the counter, feasting on her mouth and neck.

He lowered his head and, using his teeth, slipped a button on her blouse, then another and another. He teased her breast, enjoying himself and her at the same time.

"Keep them still," he demanded in a heavy breath before releasing her hands.

Butterflies fluttered in her stomach as he clasped her ankles and wrapped them around his waist. She obliged and hooked her legs firmly around him. Trent's hands and mouth teased her breasts, and she lost her thoughts of what she wanted to do. Her head fell back as she enjoyed the splendid sensations and moaned, pushing her breasts further into his hands and mouth. His fingers skated across her breast, delicately giving her nipple a squeeze.

When he pulled away, Maggie brought his head to her other breast. Focused on the feeling coursing through her body, she realized he had lifted her off the counter.

Trent carried her out of the kitchen and up the stairs. He kicked open the bedroom door and deposited her into the center of the bed. The dark brown color of the room with the darkness of night made it more challenging to see him. Her eyes adjusted, and she watched him close the door and approach the bed, taking off his clothing along the way. She wanted to kiss and explore his body, but he kept her pinned down. She wiggled beneath him so he rolled over, giving her a way to move about.

Their bodies skimmed each other's, while she kissed his neck, making her quiver. Her lips kissed his chest to his belly where he stopped her. Lifting her head to see her face, she came back to his delectable lips, knowing Trent thought of her and not of pleasing himself.

Under him again, he took his time exploring every nuance of her mouth while divesting her of her jeans. She lifted her hips off the bed to help and heard him mumbling as he sought to move away from her. Taking hold of his hips, she brought him into contact with her and sighed at their movement.

"Maggie," he said and pulled back into a kneeling position.

"Where's a condom?" she asked with his pause.

He pulled open the drawer of his nightstand, withdrew a small packet and slid the condom on as she kissed his neck.

She reached for him and pulled him to her. He slid into her wet heat and stopped. She moved slightly and prodded him, wanting him inside of her.

"Give me a second here."

Maggie rubbed his back...waiting. He kept the rhythm slow, being gentle with her, as though she were a virgin. She pulled his face to hers, connecting at the lips. He increased the rhythm and, wrapping her legs around his waist, she tumbled into an orgasm. Trent shuddered and followed her into the abyss.

He lay to the side and spooned against her back. She took slow steady breaths several times before eventually falling asleep.

She woke with his arms around her. Last night had been breathtaking in more ways than one. He had been gentle and loving, and they had had a great evening leading up to her stay.

Why did it feel so different to be with Trent than it did with Mike...or any other guy? She enjoyed being with Trent. He didn't make her nervous like Kevin did. She wasn't looking to get involved with another man, but here she lay next to Trent in his bed.

Trent stirred before gazing into her eyes.

"Good morning," she offered.

He pulled her close and returned a good morning to her with a kiss. "Did you sleep well?"

She answered with a murmur, not wanting to face those sleepy, sexy eyes, and turned to spoon with him. At the moment, she had mixed emotions about what had transpired between them. Last night happened because she wanted it to, yet her feelings for Trent were happening too quickly. She shouldn't feel this way after being divorced for two months. It was too soon.

He pushed her hair away from her neck and kissed behind her ear. "I'm glad you stayed." He nibbled on her ear. "Why don't we shower and go for a morning ride? It's as beautiful during the morning as it is in the evening."

He kissed her, and his erection pressed against her backside. Maggie sat on the edge of the bed. "I can't stay, and you're not to go riding per doctor's orders. I need to get going. I have some things I need to take care of."

"Maggie?"

At the touch of his hand on her back, she sat straighter and pulled away. She didn't face him while he talked.

"Look at me," he said. "You're not upset about...about staying here last night, are you?"

"No. Last night was... It was special." She slid off the bed and headed for the bathroom. "I just need to get going." Glad he stayed behind in bed, she closed the bathroom door.

While in the shower, she heard him come into the room. She turned the water off, and he asked, "If it's not about last night, then what's wrong?"

"I've had a lot on my mind about the things I need to get done today." She stayed in the shower to dry off or maybe to hide.

She stepped from behind the shower door and gasped at the sight in front of her. He stood buck-naked shaving at the sink. It had been awhile since she'd shared a bathroom with a man.

With the towel wrapped around her, she walked into the bedroom and gathered her clothes scattered throughout the room to get dressed.

"They're downstairs on the kitchen floor," he said as she searched for her shoes.

"Oh...yeah, thanks," she said, warming, not from the shower, but from remembering their encounter in the kitchen.

He strolled toward the door and moved closer. "Maggie."

At the sound of his voice saying her name, her heart skipped, and her stomach knotted. She faced him and weakened in the legs.

He wrapped his arm around her waist and pulled her into his bare chest. "I'll call you."

Trent kissed her. Slow, steady, deeply. The kind of kiss that had meaning behind it. The kind of kiss that sucked all life out of you. The kind of kiss that was more than what she expected or needed right now.

She stood a few moments to regain her strength. With an urge to stay, she had to leave and think things through.

Maggie said goodbye, opened the door, and disappeared into the hall.

Chapter Fourteen

Trent stood in front of the open refrigerator in an attempt to find something to eat. Nothing appealed to him. He wanted to go for a ride with Maggie. He closed the refrigerator door with more force than he meant to as bottles rattled their protest within.

He snatched a bagel from the bread drawer and decided to go for that morning ride. Regardless of doctor's orders. He popped the bagel in the microwave to warm and ate it as he left through the back door for the barn.

Majestic lifted his head as Trent entered the barn and gave him a whinny and stomp. "It's okay, boy," he said, approaching the horse calmly. "Let's go for a ride. I need a little fresh air."

The two trotted into the pasture leading to the woods on the trail they had created through years of use. Trent and Majestic had produced several paths, but this one would take Trent to his favorite spot along the river.

His thoughts wandered to Maggie and their night together. Did she truly have things to do today? Did she regret what happened between them?

He didn't want to rush things with her as he had with the other women from his past. She had given herself to him last night, and he had been gentle with her, taking his time. Maggie was different and special. His heart beat twice its speed when with her. She had a past where she had been hurt. Money had been important to the other women he dated, but not to Maggie. Although she came from money, he knew it didn't mean the world to her because she worked and worked hard.

He sat atop the stallion and watched the water rush over the rocky riverbeds, creating rapids and then on to the slower paced flow of the river. Had he passed over those rougher waters when he moved to Florida? Were the calm waters in front of him a sign to move on with his life?

Yes, the time had come, and Maggie was the one for him to share his future. She opened her heart, and by doing so, his opened up too with no fear of damage.

He bent over and put his face to Majestic's ear. "I think we need to court Ms. Carlisle the old-fashioned way."

As if in understanding, the Paint whinnied and shook his head.

Trent laughed. Since the party at the house, he'd learned about her family and growing up in Texas. Still, he didn't know the story about the scar on her face. It would come with time, when she was ready.

His heartbeat accelerated at the realization of how much he missed Maggie and wished she could be there to share the moment and place with him, but as his wife.

The notion that he wanted their relationship to become much more stunned him. However, would Maggie allow that to happen? Would her heart open up to him and accept love again?

He thought it—love. Could he love her and have those feelings again after Janet destroyed them? After a while he decided, yes, it was love.

~ * ~

In his office, Trent answered the phone while perusing paperwork. "Rolling Rock Boarding and Breeding Ranch. Trent Randall speaking."

"Mr. Randall, this is Steven Carlisle."

"Mr. Carlisle, what can I do for you?" He wondered why Maggie's father would be calling. His nerves went on heightened alert.

"I'm planning a little trip and will be your way next weekend. I'd like to take a tour of the ranch and your operations. How does next Friday work for you?"

Trent glanced at his calendar and answered as professionally as possible, without quavering, "Fine, sir."

"Good, and I plan on paying a surprise visit to see my daughter. It's come to my attention my daughter has a man in her life, so you and I can talk then. Bye now, Mr. Randall."

"Excuse me?" The phone line went dead, and he set the phone into the cradle. "Shit! How in the hell did he find out? Chloe. The man has impeccable timing, that's for sure. So much for an old-fashioned courtship." He leaned back in his chair. Maybe this visit could work in his favor.

Trent smiled and relaxed about Steven's visit. If her father knew about their relationship, it might make things easier. He would also need to keep the visit quiet from Maggie. Her father had said a 'surprise' visit. She'd be surprised all right.

~ * ~

Home from work Thursday, Maggie checked for messages as she opened the patio door and windows. The fresh, ocean air flowed through the house. The salty breeze was welcoming after having been stuck inside the stale hospital environment. As she approached the stairs leading to her room, a knock came from the deck.

"Kevin?" Maggie stood stunned at the screen door.

He had his pant legs rolled and wore no shoes.

"I went for a walk." He opened the patio door and stepped inside. "And thought I'd stop and say hello."

He pulled her flush against his body, and his lips made contact with hers.

She pushed on his chest and forced him back. "What do you think you're doing? I've told you I don't want to see you anymore." She wiped away what she could of the kiss.

"Maggie, what did I do to make you this mad? I thought we had something good between us."

"I'm actually seeing someone else, and it's serious." A lie she didn't mind telling. She stepped outside and into the public eye.

"When did this happen?"

111

"I've been seeing him for the last couple of weeks on and off, and it's gotten more serious the last couple of days. Kevin, I told you I don't want to see you anymore. If you don't stop harassing me, I'll go to the police."

"Okay, I'm leaving." Kevin turned and walked down the stairs.

Maggie waited until he was out of her sight before going inside and locking the screen door. It wouldn't stop someone from entering if they really wanted to get in, but it would have prevented Kevin from sneaking into the house.

Upstairs she rinsed her mouth thoroughly with mouthwash before she changed out of the scrubs. Who does he think he is? Walking into her house without an invitation and then kissing her. Eeew!

~ * ~

Trent rushed outside at the sound of an approaching vehicle Saturday evening. He stepped off the porch as a car screeched to a halt. It wasn't Maggie, but some of the racing crew. Disappointment set in.

"What are you doing here?" he asked, not caring if he sounded inhospitable. He hoped they'd leave.

"We came to take a swim. You don't mind, do you?" Harry asked, jumping out from the car with a towel.

"I'm expecting company. I don't have time to entertain you three," he replied, still hoping they'd get the picture.

"No need. We only wanted to cool off. It sure is steamy today," Lance said with his towel in hand.

"Suit yourselves." The words escaped his mouth as another car approached.

Maggie pulled in next to Harry's car. Ignoring the whistles from the guys, he opened her door. "Let's get out of here." He took her hand and hustled her toward the barn.

"Well, hello to you, too."

"Sorry, I want to avoid the audience," he quickly replied at the puzzlement clear in her voice. He took a fleeting glance back, while she struggled to keep up with his quick, long strides.

He closed the barn door behind them and pulled her into an

embrace. He didn't know how long he could go without touching her. She stood stiff in his arms. "I missed you," he said before releasing her from the hug.

"Really?"

"Yes, *really*, so you can lose the smug smile." They went to their respective horses. He stepped in to see Majestic after he grabbed his tack. "How're you doing today?" Trent asked his prize possession.

He knew Maggie could hear him but didn't care. Then he heard her talking to Blue, too. They both crooned to the horses, while they prepped for the ride.

"Has Majestic always had that stall?" she asked, tightening the saddle strap.

"No. I switched him this morning. He and Blue enjoy each other's company, so I moved him across the way." Maggie stood right outside his stall door. "Ready?"

"Yes, would you like me to wait outside?" She opened the doors.

"Nope, I'm about ready here." He walked through the barn doors and swung up into his saddle. Trent pulled back on the reins, bringing Majestic to a halt at the edge of the yard as Maggie swung up on Blue. "You take the lead."

"Which way do you want to go?"

"Why not let Blue lead you?" he said as his horse fell into step next to her mount.

They walked for a few minutes before she pushed her horse to a gallop. Surprised when she dashed off, he pushed Majestic into a gallop to follow.

She stopped by the creek, and Trent dismounted.

"Are you enjoying yourself?" He lifted her off Blue.

"It's beautiful here, Trent." Her face glowed and warmed his heart.

"I love it here." He wrapped his arms around her waist.

"I thought racing was your passion."

"A rancher first and foremost. I didn't know much about racing and still have a lot to learn. I've surrounded myself with people who know their stuff in that area. What I know is horses and land."

"You had quite a spread in Colorado." She turned and faced him.

"What made you finally sell?"

"My mother. She encouraged the move. After my grandfather's passing, she encouraged moving as much as Janet encouraged selling."

"You miss your grandfather, don't you?" Maggie asked and focused on the river.

"Yup."

"I'm sorry for your loss."

"Why do people say that when you tell them you've lost somebody?" Trent asked philosophically, and stepped out of the embrace.

"Because you sound as if you really miss him." She leaned against a tree.

He rested his palms on either side of her head on the trunk of the tree and, leaning forward, whispered, "I do miss him, everyday." Their lips caressed.

The kiss light and casual, her fingers wrapped through his belt loops as she pulled him closer. On her cue, he deepened the kiss while his hands cradled her head.

Not sure which of them moaned, Trent pulled away before things got out of hand. She yanked him back, flush against her.

"Tell me what you want, Maggie." He wanted her to know she controlled the situation.

"This," she replied. Her hands caressed his chest before she slid them around to his backside. She grabbed his ass and pulled him into her.

This time he did the moaning. He wanted to slow things a bit but wanted her to be in charge. He needed to make sure the next time they made love she would not regret it as she'd seemed to the other night.

"Maggie…" He pulled his head back to peer into her eyes.

"Trent," she replied with a mischievous grin on her face.

"Let's ride," he countered and pulled away.

He strode to his horse and hoped he could ride in his aroused state. The last time he'd ridden with an erection was when he was a teenager. To alleviate the situation, baseball statistics ran through his head.

They rode in silence until they came to a small lake.

"This is picturesque–a serene little lake in your own back yard," she called out to Trent who lagged behind.

He rounded the curve where the lake sat nestled amongst a stand of trees, hidden from view.

"Do you want to swim?" He smiled atop his horse.

"What about the gators?"

"I don't think they'd mind sharing the lake with you."

"You're kidding, right?"

"Actually, I don't know. Never thought to check it out. I've got a perfectly good pool to swim in...where I can see what's in it." Her eyes grew big and round with eyebrows raised. Her mouth hung open, unsure whether he joked or not. "Don't worry. I don't think the gators come this far in. At least I've never seen them around here."

She led her horse around the lake and back into open land, coaxing Blue into a gallop. Trent made a slight attempt to catch her but gave up on the chase.

He reigned in his horse to a stop a few inches away before nearly running into her as he rounded the barn. She sat atop her mare and smiled like the Cheshire cat.

"You're looking awfully smug." He trotted around her and dismounted before going through the open barn door.

"What took you so long to get here?" She slid out of her saddle and followed suit.

"I stopped to take a nap." He rolled with the punches. They each took hold of their currycombs.

"A nap huh? I didn't realize you got tired so easily. You look like you're in good shape. I guess it's a façade."

Trent glanced at Maggie, brushing Blue. It appeared she found currying as therapeutic as he did.

"Steaks again okay?" He leaned on the stall door. He had pulled two from the freezer before breakfast.

"Sure. Why don't you get the grill going and I'll be along shortly."

Trent returned to the house, glad to see the gang had gone home.

Chapter Fifteen

Maggie realized by the silence that they had the house to themselves. Trent worked at the grill and drank a glass of water. She wondered about his choice of drink and decided it was time to make a further inquiry of sorts.

"Can I help with anything?" she asked approaching him.

"Nope, everything is set. Can I get you a drink?"

"A cold beer would be great." She'd never seen him drink more than one beer. Why?

She finished her beer and went inside to retrieve another one before the steaks were done cooking. She took a drink as she approached the patio.

"Are you driving home, or am I taking you?" Anyone else would have thought nothing of how he asked, but his tone was too nonchalant.

Bingo! She didn't care for the seriousness reflected in his tone. "I'm driving, and I won't be drinking anymore. What's with the attitude?" She joined him at the table. He had everything dished up on their plates.

"I don't believe a person should drink excessively then be driving." He cut into his steak, taking a large chunk and shoved it in his mouth.

"Bullshit. There's more to it." She cut into her filet and softened her voice. "Something involving alcohol happened in your life, and you're taking it out on me, again." Not a big deal to her, but it was to Trent because of the way he reacted. She realized she wanted a relationship with Trent, but needed to understand what troubled him.

"Again?" he asked with puzzlement and stuck in another large bite of his steak.

She gave him a don't-you-remember look. "Yes, the block party."

With no kind of a response and not wanting to push too hard, they ate a short time in silence.

"What happened, Trent?"

"I told you, my father is an alcoholic." Short and to the point. No feeling in the words spoken.

"I'm not an alcoholic, *or* like your father." He had no right to insinuate she was like his father. "Yes, I do enjoy a drink here and there and sometimes more than one, but that doesn't make me an alcoholic."

"I know, but I get concerned when it involves people I care for." Taking her hand, Trent added, "And Maggie, I care about you."

She soaked in his last words before asking, "Where does he live?"

"I don't talk to him." He released her hand. "End of story." He took the last bite of his steak.

"There's more to the story though. It's affected your life to the point you're very aware of what the people around you are drinking." She reached out and thoughtfully touched his forearm.

"End of story," he reiterated and clenched his jaw. Wisely, but frustrated, she let the subject drop.

His face relaxed within the short time they finished dinner. He stood up and asked, "Would you like dessert?"

He cared about her and her for him. Maggie couldn't fight the need to be with him any longer. She got out of her chair and pulled him close. "What I want for dessert won't be found in the kitchen. Let's take care of this mess and make another one upstairs."

"Your dessert sounds much better than what I had in mind."

They both put their dinner items on the large serving tray and headed for the house. She opened the patio door, but before letting him through said, "I wasn't planning on driving home."

Slowly she took off her top in a striptease fashion, making Trent do a double take. She headed into the entry as he quickly, but nimbly, slid the tray on the counter. He captured her in his arms as they approached the bottom of the staircase where he spun her around and took possession of her mouth. Her body yearned for him. Her head whirled. Her heart opened.

~ * ~

The call came shortly after nine. Livid, Kevin told Ryan to stay at the ranch until he arrived and made the two-hour drive to Lake Pine. Parking next to his informer, his fists formed balls as he found out Maggie still hadn't left and darkness covered the land.

He let his guy go. He clutched a pair of binoculars, gripping them tightly. Nothing, the house lay in pitch darkness, and her car remained parked out front. She wouldn't be going home until morning. Spinning the Jag around, he headed for home.

Early Sunday morning he parked at the public beach lot and walked along the beach to monitor Maggie's house. Not knowing for sure if she came home, he sat with anticipation to catch her leaving her house rather than returning.

Kevin believed his friendship with her could be better, if only she would return his calls. He thought about Mike. Mike threw his life away, throwing Maggie away too. If Mike had kept his end of the bargain, Kevin wouldn't have had to follow through with his threats. But then again, it brought Maggie to him, where he could get his hands on her. All over her body.

The sheer thought of her body brought a grin to his face. He couldn't wait to hold her naked in his bed.

Her garage door opened, she pulled in, and the smile disappeared from his face. She'd stayed the night.

So, her relationship with 'cowboy' is serious.

He had seen enough and made the call. Kevin finished with the florist, dialed another number and waited.

"Sergeant Fritz."

"Can you talk?" he asked annoyed.

"For a moment. What's wrong?"

"I'm about to confront Maggie and need you to keep your ears open for the next week or so. I'm going to need to know of any contact she may make with the department."

"What's going on?"

"Just do as you're asked. No questions."

"Okay, I'll let you know."

He hung up, waited and watched for the flower delivery. Not until she accepted the arrangement did he approach the house. He walked up to the patio door not catching a glimpse of Maggie.

Kevin knocked and waited for her to answer. He looked to the beach and struggled to keep his anger at bay while waiting.

~ * ~

Maggie tanned on the deck when the doorbell jarred her from her state of relaxation. At the front door stood the flower delivery guy with a bouquet. Accepting them with a smile, she set them on the counter and pulled the card nestled amongst the long-stemmed red roses.

The card said, 'Love Kevin,' What the hell was that supposed to mean? Can't the man get a clue?

"Ugh." She crumpled the card. "Why can't he take no for an answer?" She closed the box and deposited the box and flowers into the trash. "Good riddance."

She went back outside and made the decision, if Kevin called or sent any more flowers, she would go to the police. She couldn't let this situation with him go on any longer.

The phone startled her.

"Good morning," came from the other end of the line.

"Good morning." The sound of Trent's voice eased the tension from her shoulders enough that she lay back in the lounge chair to soak in the late morning sun.

"What do you have planned for your last day off?"

"What did you have in mind?" She thought of his hands on her, and her body warmed internally.

"A late lunch, with a walk on the beach afterwards."

"What time?"

"I'll pick you up around three."

"Sounds good." She anticipated spending more time with Trent before he had to leave for any more out of town races.

"I'll see you then."

Maggie dialed Chloe's cell phone. "Hey, stranger," she replied with Chloe's answer.

"What do you mean stranger? I was just there, and I've been very busy playing catch-up in the office."

"Believe it or not, I've missed having you around. Are you sure you don't want to move here? You'd be closer to Chad then. Speaking of, how are things going between you two?"

"I've talked to him a few times since I got home, but we're both so busy, it's been difficult. You didn't call me to find out about my relationship. Something's going on. What gives?"

Maggie didn't answer so Chloe took a guess. "Have you and Trent slept together? Is *that* what's going on?"

"Yes and no," she replied coolly.

"Yes and no? Which one is it?" There was excitement in Chloe's voice. "Or are we talking about two different things?"

"Both."

"Okay, I'm confused. Talk."

"Yes, I've slept with Trent." She walked into the house and slid the screen door closed.

"You don't regret sleeping with him, do you?"

"No. It was nice to be with a man again." In the kitchen, she opened and stared into the fridge. "One who is actually sensitive to a woman's needs."

"So, if it's not Trent, then what is it?"

Silence.

"Kevin."

"Kevin?" Chloe sounded confused.

"Yes, Kevin is the problem." She pulled out the pitcher of iced tea, some sliced deli turkey and a block of cheese. "He won't stop pestering me. I've told him I don't want to see him."

"Why doesn't he leave you alone then?"

"I guess he thinks he still has a snowball's chance in hell, that's why." She opened a kitchen cupboard and removed a box of crackers.

"Did you do anything to make him think otherwise?"

"No! *God, no!* He did the maneuvering, and I kept pushing him away." In another cupboard, she hauled out a plate and glass and poured a glass of tea.

"How's he pursuing you?"

"He stopped by once, and I keep getting flowers from him." Maggie placed a few pieces of turkey on the plate and withdrew a knife for the cheese from the knife block. "I just got a dozen long-stemmed red roses from him and the card said, Love, Kevin."

"You've got to be kidding. You threw them away, didn't you?"

"Of course. I swear there's more to what he knows, and it gives me the creeps."

"Stay away from him. If he keeps bothering you, you need to go to the police. Especially if you think he's linked to Mike."

"Trust me, I will." She laid the cheese slices on her plate, deposited the knife in the sink, and returned everything to the fridge.

"Does Trent know about this?"

"He knows about the flowers, but not the full extent of it. I can't tell him because of the whole Mike thing. Listen, I need to go. Someone's knocking on the door."

Maggie walked into the living room and approached the patio door. What the hell? "Kevin! What are you doing here?"

"Since you haven't been answering my calls," he said, his voice business-like but tinged with mischief. "I decided to make a personal one. I want to talk to you."

"Actually..." Chills covered her body, and she shivered. "I have a lot to do today, and I'm not comfortable with you being here. I've told you that before, but you seem to ignore what I want."

He once more ignored her request to leave, slid the door open and entered. She became acutely aware of her surroundings.

"I'll make it quick." He flashed a grin, while his eyes roamed up and down her bikini-clad body.

This was what she got for not locking the screen door, again. "What do you need to talk to me about?" She quickly snatched the lightweight throw lying over the back of the chair to use as a cover up.

He glanced around the room, searching for the flowers.

"Make it quick." She stopped him, aware he was too far into the room now.

"I want some answers. Where were you last night?" His smile became a sneer, his voice rough.

"I don't think that's any of your business." She made an effort to say it firmly and backed away.

"Where were you last night?" He ground out the words through clenched teeth.

"With a friend." Her stomach knotted.

He inched closer.

"What's this *friend's* name?" he asked with an edge of impatience in his voice.

"Kevin, I don't think..." she began to say as she stepped further away.

"Who were you with?" His voice raised an octave.

"Trent Randall."

"What did you two do?" He snarled, again approaching nearer.

"I don't think you..."

"What did you do?" he asked with a roar and continued to inch closer.

Maggie maneuvered to the patio door and stepped outside. She decided arguing would be a waste of time and only anger him more. "I went riding and had dinner."

Kevin followed, eyed her from top to bottom, and back to her face. He took several deep breaths, exhaled slowly then sauntered to where she stood by the outer rail.

"I'm going to give you two choices. You'll need to decide which choice you're going to make." He fixed her with a level stare.

"Choices? I've made my choice, and it doesn't involve you."

He slithered closer, allowing only an inch of space between them. "I think you'd better listen to what I have to say before you make a decision." His voice was hushed but gruff. He positioned his arms around her.

She cringed as she was pinned against the railing. The scent of his cologne inundated her senses. Instantly her head ached, and her sinuses clogged.

"I know for a fact you did more than go riding and have dinner. You stayed the night." His nose skimmed hers. He was going to kiss her.

She swallowed the lump in her throat.

"Now, your first choice." He pulled his face away from hers but kept her against the rail. "The one I prefer, we're a couple. As in you and me, dating. Your second, and final choice, you supply me with things I need and want from the hospital."

"What could I possibly supply you with from the hospital?" Maggie struggled to control her quavering voice.

"There are certain drugs I could use, and you can get them for me. But only if you decide to go that route. Personally, I'd like you to be mine, but *you* will ultimately make the choice."

She lifted and shrugged her shoulders back as the hair stood up on her neck.

"And what if I don't want to do either?" Now she knew the connection between him and Mike. Her skin became clammy. Her stomach felt as though it were in her throat.

"Maybe it won't be your pretty face that gets cut or a simple boating mishap this time."

"Did you cause Team Seahorse's boating accident?" Her voice was that of a child's. She had to ask. She had to know.

"If I had, you can be assured Trent wouldn't have lived."

"Mike stole the drugs from the hospital for you. You're the reason behind this scar and my divorce. Why would I do either of these things for you? I'm not Mike and won't be your puppet."

"You have a choice to make, or this time a family member will get hurt. Maybe something happens to someone's ranch or…"

"Okay…enough…I get the picture," she said alarmed.

"I'm glad you do." He leaned into her and whispered, "I'll call you soon to find out what you decide." Forcefully, he took possession of her mouth. "Oh, by the way…don't try contacting the Sheriff's Office. I have connections there. I'd hate to hear you've made an effort to contact them." Kevin kept his calm and sauntered down the deck stairs to the beach.

Maggie stood shaking for a moment before she rushed inside to close and lock the door behind her. She swiftly climbed the stairs to her room, went to her patio door and onto her balcony. Kevin strolled along the beach a short distance before he disappeared.

She hustled into the bathroom and peered out the window to where she assumed his car would be. Not seeing him, she wondered where he parked. She continued her vigil until a short time later saw his Jag drive past. She could not believe it; he had been watching her all this time. Chloe had been right to raise suspicion, but Maggie had been quick to dismiss it, living on the public beach. How long had he been watching her?

Why didn't she lock the screen? Too late at this point, she faced a horrid decision. Panic flooded her. Her heart hammered in her chest. Her breathing quickened. What the hell was she going to do? He'd given her two choices, neither of which she wanted to choose.

She needed to escape. The house overwhelmed her, so she went back outside. Normally when her bare feet hit the sand, the tension disappeared, but not today. Last night had been so wonderful, and now Kevin had to show up.

She found a spot not far from the house and sat. What to do? She didn't like being with Kevin, yet she could not, and would not, steal drugs for him from the hospital.

Her only choice was to end things with Trent to protect him and become involved with Kevin. She shuddered and recalled his parting comments about going to the police. Her stomach roiled at the notion of what had transpired at the house, and she went back onto her deck, collapsing on the closest chair she came to.

Maggie thought about the possibility of stealing drugs from the hospital. How stupid could she have been? Kevin and Mike *were* more than business friends. Now Kevin was going to use her like he had Mike.

Chapter Sixteen

Maggie opened the door, and Trent held a single, yellow rose. "Thank you," she said with a smile and gestured him to enter. Her nerves from Kevin's recent visit diminished slightly with his arrival. "So, where are we going for lunch?"

"Turtle's. Thought we could go some place casual."

"Let me place this beautiful rose in a vase then I'm ready to go."

She got into his pick-up but not without glancing about to see if Kevin was in the area. Not seeing his car anywhere, she continued to be observant while Trent drove.

"Everything okay?"

"Fine. When I'm driving, I don't get the chance to look around."

"I know what you mean. On the ride home from our last race, when I couldn't drive, the scenery and small conversations were all I had. It was nice for a change. I did sleep for a few short spells. Probably a good thing I didn't drive."

With silence between them, she continued to glimpse in the side mirror but didn't notice any familiar cars following them. She breathed a sigh of relief.

Kevin's car was absent when Trent pulled into Turtle's parking lot, and that put her in a temporary state of relaxation. He opened her door, and she took his hand, lacing her fingers in his. She continued to hold and touch his hand once seated at their table, appreciating his gentle kindness.

Turtle's hadn't changed much over the years. She liked the mix of colors, giving her a sense of Key West and the smell of good food mingled with the salty air. She had gone many times with her parents, which made it more comfortable to be there with Trent.

She gazed from the upper outdoor deck at the waterway while waiting for their food to arrive. A couple of boats tied at the docks bobbed in the water.

"Have you been enjoying your time off?" Trent asked, his effort to bring her back to him.

"It's been nice."

"How do you come home and sleep when you work the overnight shift?"

"Being by the ocean can be relaxing, and you get used to the hours." She brushed her fingers through her hair and pulled it forward.

"Don't phone calls or the doorbell bother you?"

"Not often, but sometimes I sleep with earplugs. You learn how to deal with it."

Their food arrived, and she ate a few bites of her salad, but Kevin's visit had curbed her appetite. "I talked to my mother, and she said my father might be stopping by to visit." She pushed the shrimp and mandarin oranges around her bowl to mingle with lettuce, mangos, and dried cranberries.

"Will I get to meet him?"

"I don't know. He may or may not stop by the beach house. My mother didn't know for sure. I'd love for you to meet him if you're here and not at a racing event. He'd like you."

"How will you introduce me?" He took her hand and gave it an affectionate squeeze.

She removed her hand from his and pushed her plate to the side. "I would tell him you're a really good friend. Someone I've been able to talk to and do things with."

"What's wrong?" He made the effort to take her hand again, but she wouldn't let him.

"If you don't mind, I'd like to go back to my place. I don't feel good."

"Sure. Let me take care of the bill." Trent motioned for the waitress. "Is your food okay?"

"It's fine. My stomach is off a bit."

The ride home was quiet, but she let him hold her hand. She would catch him occasionally peering at her. They neared her house, and she became very vigilant of the vehicles parked on the road. No Jag. He pulled into her driveway and parked the truck. She entered the garage code and made her way for the house door.

Trent caught up to her and seized her wrist. "Wait a minute."

Maggie turned her head, glanced at her wrist, stared at Trent, and tranquilly asked, "What?"

"Are you okay?" He released his grip and took her hand. "You've been distracted ever since we left Turtle's and more when we got closer to your place. What's going on?"

"I'd like to walk along the beach, but first I need to check my phone messages."

"On our walk," he released her hand, "I want you to talk to me." He followed her through the open door.

Relieved and comforted to find no messages, she let go of the breath she had been holding. She turned to face Trent. "Why don't we take our shoes off?"

"You said back at the restaurant you didn't feel good."

"I'll feel better when we're done walking." She hoped.

In the living room, they both slipped their shoes off at the patio door and stepped into the early evening air. Clear skies and a slight breeze off the Gulf had her tilting her head to the sun. She inhaled, and the sea salt in the atmosphere inundated her senses.

"Oh, that feels so good." She sighed at the coolness of the sand between her toes. She accepted the hand he offered.

"What's wrong, Maggie?" he asked firmly, but with concern.

"It's funny how both you and Chloe know when something isn't right with me." It was time to open up a little to him.

"Chloe?" His tone grew casual and more relaxed.

"Yeah, I called her, and she sensed it. I'll tell you the same thing I told her." She quickened her pace. She wanted to run away to some far off place, safe where Kevin would never be able to find her.

"Maggie, slow down. This is supposed to be relaxing. What did you tell Chloe?"

"Kevin is still pursuing me."

"What?" he yelled and efficiently pulled her to a stop. He faced her and asked, "What do you mean? I thought you told him you weren't interested."

"Trent, please...please lower your voice." She perused the beach to see who might be watching them.

His hand slipped from hers, and he took several steps away before he turned to face her. He was hurt, and her heart fell to the pit of her stomach.

"You did tell him you weren't interested, didn't you?" he asked with his voice lowered, but brusque.

Maggie took the few steps to join him and when she reached to take his hand, he accepted it and gave a gentle squeeze.

"I did tell him. But he continues to call and has sent flowers, telling me he misses me and wants to see me."

"Have you seen him lately? Or talked to him?"

"No. Let's go back." Not about to open a can of worms on the public beach, she would wait to tell him about the situation with Kevin.

"Are we a couple? Do you want to be a part of this relationship and have it be more than a friendship?"

Maggie stopped, wrapped her arms around his neck and affectionately kissed him on the lips. "This is more than a friendship, and I won't be dating anyone else if that's what you're wondering."

"Why would you tell your father this is a friendship if it's more than that?"

"I guess I'm not ready to tell anyone yet. I'm happy when I'm with you and don't want anything to spoil what I have. If that means I keep our relationship to myself, then I will." She kissed him again, sliding her arms around his waist, holding him in an embrace. "With my divorce two months old, I'm finding it difficult to believe this is happening. That there's a possibility..." She stopped short of saying the 'L' word and quickly added, "I am not ready to advertise this relationship and hope you understand."

They walked back in silence, holding hands and, every once in a while, sharing gentle squeezes. At the patio door, Trent pulled her into his arms and kissed her. His soul poured into hers. Maggie peered into his soft eyes, not dark like they had been on the beach.

"Will you stay tonight?" she asked.

"Don't you work tomorrow?"

"I work at ten. So, will you stay?"

He swept her into his arms and carried her up the stairs. He laid her tenderly on the bed. She sat upright, unbuttoned his shirt and spread it open before kissing around his navel.

She stood and pulled the shirt down his shoulders, holding it around his elbows so he couldn't move. Kissing his chest, she worked her way lower down the trail of hair leading to the top of his pants.

She yanked the shirt off, letting it fall to the floor, but as her hands went to undo his pants, he pulled them away and brought them back up to his chest. Kissing her, he struggled to find the zipper on her dress, and when he did locate it, he slowly lowered it. His lips skated from hers, to her ear and then on to her neck, a hot wave swept into her belly.

He slid the straps from her shoulders, kissing her right one after the strap fell. His lips skimmed across her collarbone and between her breastbones to the left side. Her dress slithered to her hips. He stared at her white lace demi-bra with reverence.

The dress drifted to the floor. The matching white lace thong still hugged her hips. He cupped her bottom with his hands and lifted her to kiss her lips.

Maggie felt his erection when she undid his pants and tugged them down to drop to the floor. She sighed with approval. He wore nothing underneath his jeans.

He wasn't the only one ready for action. The moment he had swept her into his arms Maggie had been warm with want, and when he had undressed her, the need grew. She stroked him while kissing his chest and murmured, "I want you."

Trent glanced to the king-sized bed covered with pillows and back at Maggie. Understanding his thoughts, she walked to the head of the bed, threw back the covers and pushed the pile of pillows to the floor.

The last pillows fell, and he seized her from behind. This took her by surprise.

He kissed her back, nipping here and there while he worked on her bra. She assisted him as he struggled to get the bra unhooked. She pressed against his chest, as his hand slid between her thighs. His erection pressed against her backside.

Trent pushed the hair off her neck and kissed her. He skimmed his hand into her panties, inserting a finger into her wetness. She moaned his name and tipped her head back to rest on his shoulder while he continued to explore. Her breath heavy with desire, he brought her to a heightened state but stopped.

He turned her around, kissing her before he eased her back to lie on the bed and removed her underwear. He kissed every inch of her, from her waist back to her mouth, where she greedily took him.

She reached back to her nightstand. He leaned over, peering in the drawer, and came back with the small packet. "Let me." Her voice was husky as she took the packet from his hands.

She unwrapped the condom, straddled him and threw the wrapping to land somewhere on the floor. Slowly unrolling it down his shaft, she heard him moan and stroked his firmness. She slid up over him and guided him into her. He gave them both a moment before rolling her onto her back. She closed her eyes. He eased out, and she lifted her knees, spreading her legs for him to gain deeper entry.

"Let's roll over," she moaned.

The motion slow and steady, she picked up the pace and neared orgasm. Trent shuddered, and moments later she came falling against his torso. Her breathing intense, she kissed him before burying her face into his chest. He smelled of soap and sex.

Trent ran his hand along her rib cage, "I love touching you. Your skin's as soft as a rose petal." He sat up and pulled on the disheveled sheets to cover them up.

Maggie went back into his arms, laying her head on his chest, and he held her while they fell asleep.

~ * ~

Maggie woke in the very early morning hours and slipped into Trent's shirt. Stepping out onto the moonlit balcony, she stood at the rail and released the tears.

"Maggie?" She heard the concern in his voice coming from the bedroom.

"I'm out here," she softly answered.

His hands slid around her waist in an embrace. "What are you doing out here?"

She couldn't stand the thought of facing him. She knew her eyes would be puffy and wet and wiped away the tears. "I couldn't sleep. I thought I'd get some fresh air." She gazed out to the horizon of the ocean.

He guided her to the lounge chair where she sat next to him. He held her hand and wrapped an arm around her.

"Promise me you won't interrupt." She knew talking about her past would be difficult, but the time had come. It was only fair. He had opened up on more than one occasion with her.

"I promise."

"My cut was an accident, but happened during an act of rage. Mike, my ex-husband, was stealing and selling drugs from the pharmacy at the hospital where we worked. I never knew about it until it was too late." She paused, and kept her head bent and stared at her feet. She couldn't face him...no way. Telling him about the incident would be hard enough, but having feelings for him made it more difficult.

"I stayed home sick one day, and someone broke into the house. The guy, Rick, was searching for the drugs Mike was supposed to get for his boss. He didn't find any but found me instead. He made me call Mike at work and tell him I needed him to come home.

"When Mike arrived later, he found me held at knifepoint. He told the guy I wasn't what they wanted, and the two men shared some words."

She shivered, remembering the way her captor touched her with his hands. She touched the scar. "Mike told the guy to tell the boss he couldn't get the goods yet and was still working on it. Rick told him the boss didn't want to hear that and wanted the goods now. At that moment, I truly learned how deep Mike was into the illegal drug business and how much trouble he was in."

She shuffled her feet some more. "When Rick told Mike that's not what the boss wanted to hear, Mike attacked Rick. The knife Rick held, well, ...that's how I got the cut."

Trent's hand compressed into a tight fist. She took his hand back into hers, giving it a gentle squeeze. She needed him to remain calm. She wanted him to comfort her.

She shifted on the lounge chair and turned her back to rest on his shoulder. He wrapped his arm around her.

"I'm lucky to be alive because if the knife would've been an eighth of an inch lower..." She left the consequences to his imagination. "Well, I wouldn't be here. He would've cut the carotid artery. They told me I passed out from blood loss."

"My parents were at my bed side when I woke. I told my dad I wanted to divorce Mike, but my parents didn't understand why until later. The nurses alerted Mike, working in the pharmacy, when I awoke. He came to my room and asked me to lie to the police. I told him I would but that I didn't want to see him again." She lifted her head toward the glistening waters to catch a deep breath before continuing.

"The police questioned me at the hospital, but I couldn't lie. I told them everything I knew about the incident. Released from the hospital several days later, I stayed with my parents. What I didn't know was that the police happened to be on to Mike and had been doing surveillance. Mike went to make a delivery and got caught. He's out on a bond awaiting trial."

She peered back down at her legs and gazed at the hand she held in hers, firm, strong, caring, and loving—Trent's hand, not Mike's.

"The divorce papers were drawn up and ready for Mike to sign. He only pleaded once with me. When I told him it was either this or go to court, he signed them.

"Our house was purchased legally and not involved in the illegal activities so I got to keep it. He agreed to everything I wanted, and with no children, the divorce was settled quickly.

"I never returned to the house. I sold it as soon as I could. I stayed with my parents, and that's when I realized it was time to leave. I asked about moving here, and, well, here I am."

Trent turned her to face him and kissed her forehead. "Oh, Maggie...I'm glad you finally told me."

"There's more."

Chapter Seventeen

"More? What else could there possibly be?" Trent asked without raising his voice.

Maggie hung her head, averting her eyes from his. It was bad enough about the scar, but she knew what she was about to tell him could push him over the edge.

"I'm so sorry for not telling you earlier, but I didn't want to tell you on the beach and have you yelling."

"Yelling? Why would I yell at you? Did Mike yell at you a lot in your marriage that you think I'm going to?"

She didn't answer him, wanting to stay focused. "Kevin." Trent made a disgruntled noise, and she continued, "I've come to the conclusion, but don't have proof, that Mike was Kevin's supplier. I knew Kevin and Mike were friends through the pharmaceutical business, but I didn't know what kind of friends until he came to the house today."

Trent became rigid. She felt the muscles contracting in his forearms before he released his hands from hers.

"Kevin approached me with an ultimatum. I either steal drugs for him from the hospital, or I become involved with him, intimately."

"What?" He lifted her face to peer into her eyes. "I'm sorry, but I can't stay quiet any longer. You need to go to the police."

"I can't," she said barely a whisper. "I asked him what would happen if I chose to do neither. He told me he has connections and would find out if I went to the police. He's threatened to harm others if

134

I go to the police. Trent, I'm afraid. I've thought about calling Mike because I thought maybe, maybe he'd know what to do. I feel like I need him again and damn it, I don't. But I don't know where to turn."

She went to Trent's open arms and let him comfort her. Through tear-filled eyes, she sobbed, "I can't stand the thought of being with him, and morally I can't steal those drugs. I could live inside my own little shell for the rest of my life though if I was with him." Her body and mind relieved the pent-up anxiety in uncontrollable shaking and a flood of tears.

"I'm going to help you. Our relationship's not coming to an end because of a man who wants to bully a woman. When does he want your decision?"

"He said—he'd contact—me—within—a few days," she said between sobs and breaths.

"I want you to stop worrying about this. I'm going to take care of it. Let me deal with Kevin." Trent guided her back inside with an arm around her waist.

She crawled into bed while he closed the patio door. Trent gathered her in his arms, and they slept spooned together.

The following morning Maggie walked into the bathroom. In the mirror's reflection, she stood wearing his shirt. Last night she opened up to Trent, and relief and a sense of freedom flowed through her. She drew the cotton up to her nose and smelled his scent on it—nothing but good clean soap. Her eyes closed while inhaling. When she opened them, Trent stood there...with nothing on.

She approached his magnificent body and rested her hands on his chest. Gently taking hold of a handful of curly chest hair, she said, "Meet me in bed," and walked past him.

He captured her left butt cheek, giving it a squeeze, and she squealed. The way he touched her made her want him more.

"Remind me to thank you later for making my stay so accommodating." He joined her under the sheets. "I see you've removed my shirt."

"I didn't want anything to get in our way," she said with a smile and giggle.

~ * ~

Over the next few days, Maggie scouted the hospital and walked through the back entrance of the hospital, wanting to know as much as possible about the layout. Since she'd begun working there, she stuck with her routine and didn't snoop around. Now she needed to.

Although Trent had said he'd help her and not to worry, she had to work out her own possible solutions. The only way to do that was to be nosey. She still didn't know what drugs Kevin wanted her to get, so the more she knew the whereabouts of things, the better.

Never having observed any hidden cameras before, she wondered about their locations. Then again, she had never had a reason to be aware of them. The hospital had uniformed security personnel strolling around, so she knew there had to be cameras, too.

She paused along the back wall at the pharmacy area at the end of her shift.

"You find the pharmacy quite interesting, Ms. Carlisle?"

The sound of a deep voice made her jump and turn. She came face to face with a man in uniform.

"I've been thinking of going back to school." Although nervous, she was quick witted with her response.

"Please follow me," the security guard said and turned to walk away.

"What for?" she asked scared.

"I'll explain once we're behind closed doors."

Maggie followed, not saying another word and attempted to calm herself. The tension eased slightly with the realization she hadn't done anything—yet.

They walked the halls of the hospital and through a door that lead to more hallways and doors. Eventually he opened a door, and four desks with papers and folders on them, sat arranged like a recess game of four square. No sign of personalization on the desks led Maggie to believe the security personnel team shared this space. He motioned for her to sit. She did so but remained silent until asked a question.

"My name's Todd Shiffer. I have some questions to ask you."

She nodded and waited for him to proceed.

"We've observed you spending a good deal of time standing and watching the pharmacy."

Maggie took slow steady breaths to soothe herself.

"You've also been seen checking closets and various rooms you don't need to be inside. Can you explain this?"

"As I told you before, I've been thinking about going back to school to possibly become a pharmacist," she replied.

"Can you explain why you appear to be searching around the other places?" He scribbled notes on a notepad.

"I'm still new to the hospital and getting my bearings of where everything is located. I like to know where to go if there is an emergency or if questioned by a patient or visitor."

"We're aware of your husband's past and know you were cleared of any involvement. But know this, you have raised a watchful eye." He stood and said, "If we have any further questions for you, we'll contact you. Thank you for your time and cooperation."

"Thank you." She took his hand and hoped he couldn't feel hers quavering.

In her car, the shaking commenced, and the panic set in. There was no way in hell she would get away with this. What was she going to do? She didn't want to leave Trent. Not now. They'd grown so close. Aware of her now, hospital security would continue to observe her.

She closed the garage door after pulling in and quickly locked herself inside the house. She walked around checking every one of the doors and windows, making sure they remained locked. She didn't think Kevin would try to break in, but he'd played a role in her scarring incident so she was going to be careful.

God, what the hell was she thinking! Kevin was only thinking about himself. He'd rather have her in his bed. The mere thought of it made her want to throw up.

She needed to get some rest after a night of little sleep. Mentally and physically exhausted, she took one of her prescription sleeping aids. Lying under her covers with a book, she was dead to the outside world within ten minutes.

The phone rang and startled Maggie awake. The clock glowed past ten when she glanced over. She had been asleep for over three hours. Groggy, she grasped the phone and answered.

"Were you sleeping?"

Kevin. She was awake in an instant.

"I didn't wake you, did I?"

"No." She kept it simple. Not ready, knowing he wanted her decision.

"Too bad. I was thinking how beautiful you would be waking next to me."

"What do you want?" She pulled herself up to rest against her pillows.

"Oh, I think you know what I want. It's a matter of you telling me which one you have chosen."

"I don't know." She sat stiff on the edge of her bed. "I'm having a difficult time making a decision. I'm trying to figure out what I could do at the hospital." She took a deep breath and made a short prayer, "Please, I need more time."

"I would think you've had enough time to make a choice, and it sounds as if you have."

"I…"

"Then again, maybe you're having second thoughts if you're telling me you need more time." He sighed with a brief pause. "You have until Monday morning. I'll be calling for your answer."

"Thanks." Asshole.

"Looking forward to it," and he hung up.

Maggie lay back in bed, wondering how this would all work out. Exhausted and feeling the effects of the sleeping pills, she closed her eyes and let the medication do its work.

~ * ~

Kevin no sooner than hung up from his call to Maggie and the phone buzzed. His hospital contact displayed in the screen. "Shaw," he answered.

"Security had her in for questioning."

"What for?"

"She's been hanging around the pharmacy and snooping through closets and other rooms."

"What else?" This information didn't please him.

"That's pretty much it. They're watching her closely though."

"Thanks for the call," he said and hung up.

So, Maggie's looking into things which could only mean she doesn't want to go with the other option. But, on second thought, having been caught by security could work in *his* favor.

Maybe he needed to send her a message to reconfirm his threats, let her know he wasn't blowing smoke up her ass, and make it smoke elsewhere.

Chapter Eighteen

Before the sun crested the horizon Friday morning, Trent had everything set to go. He had Maggie on his mind for several reasons. One, of course, was Kevin. The second, today Trent would meet Maggie's father, Steven, for the first time. He had made sure the lawn service came in the morning and made his own rounds through every building on the ranch before going for a short ride on Majestic.

Upon returning from his ride, he went to the garage where the team worked on the boat. They'd fixed the boat in under two week's time to have it ready for North Carolina.

They went through the list of things needed. Certain decals had to be visible to the public and others properly displayed based on the racing guidelines. They needed to have their 'uniforms' and those had to have the necessary patches on them. Trent headed for the house after he talked to Lance and Alan.

The doorbell rang, and taking a deep breath, Trent stood from the office chair and stretched. This was it. Maggie's father had arrived. They were about to meet—face to face.

He opened the door. Maggie's father stood a good six feet tall and had short gray hair with some black peeking through.

The tanned, physically fit man extended his hand. "Steven Carlisle."

"Sir," he said shaking his hand, "Trent Randall. It's a pleasure to meet you."

"Please call me Steven." He had a deep southern Texas voice. One with authority.

"Any troubles finding your way?" He started asking questions and engaging in conversation to quell his nerves.

"Nope." Steven perused the grounds and gestured with his hands out. "Mighty impressive place you have here. Several of my associates living in the area had highly recommended your ranch, saying it's the best in the state."

"Glad to hear. I hope you find it to be everything you expected. Why don't I show you around?"

"Great." Steven cupped a firm hand on his shoulder. "Then you can tell me more about you and my daughter."

"We're good friends. What's there to say?"

"I'm no fool, young man. I know you're more than a *friend* to Maggie, but we'll talk more 'bout that later. Right now, let's have a look 'round and see what you've got here."

"Why don't we start this way then?" Pride and nervousness raced through his body.

They walked the grounds of Rolling Rock and the garage for Team Seahorse. Steven insisted on seeing the boat and Trent's home. Normally he didn't give tours of his home, but this wasn't a normal situation. The tour of the house ended in Trent's office.

"My wife learned about you during one of her many conversations with my daughter. Tell me, what's the status of this relationship?"

"Can I get you anything to drink?" Trent asked, hoping to avoid answering Steven's questions about his relationship with Maggie. He knew how she felt about their relationship and how little she wanted to reveal to people.

"No, thank you, but I would like an answer to my question, son."

"I will tell you this, I like your daughter...a lot. I'm not sure what she has told your wife, but I think you should talk to your daughter."

Steven didn't answer for a moment, and Trent's stomach flipped like a pancake.

"Not quite the answer I was lookin' for, but I'll accept and respect it. I'd like you to join us for dinner tomorrow evening. Come to the house about six. I've made reservations at the Columbia. Right now, I

141

have a daughter I'd like to visit."

"She's going to be very happy to see you, sir." Trent escorted Steven outside to his truck. "It was a pleasure to meet you, Steven." The men shook hands.

"I'll see you tomorrow," Steven said and nodded his head.

Trent waved as Steven drove away. Under his breath, he said, "Tomorrow," and inhaled deeply with a sigh of relief.

Suddenly, the smell of smoke inundated his nostrils. Quickly he walked the grounds searching the buildings and ran into Juan. "Where's that smell coming from? Where's the smoke?"

"I can't find it, sir."

"Do we have any riders on the trails?" Nervousness turned into alarm.

"Only Jake go for a ride."

"Juan, you stay by the barns." Trent threw a bridle and reins on Majestic, "and make sure if you discover a fire that it doesn't endanger the animals. We need to keep the horses safe." He hopped bareback atop his mount. "Do you have your cell phone?"

"Yes, sir."

"Listen for it. I may call for help," and he took off in the direction his nose led him.

He glanced to the treetops, fearing to see dark smoke. "Jake," he yelled and turned his horse around going back the way he had come in order to go down another trail. "Jake," he hollered again.

Smoke lingered in the air, and Trent didn't waste time. He dialed Juan's cell and barked the orders, "Call the fire department. We've got a wildfire on Rocky, the northwest trail."

"Yes sir, I call now."

"Has Jake come back?"

"No, sir."

"I'm going to find him," he said and hung up. He dialed Jake's cell phone. No answer. He yelled out into the smoke-filled path, "Jake! Jake, are you out there?" He stopped as the smoke got thicker the farther he went on the trail. Panic began to settle over him.

Trent squinted at the sting of the smoke and pulled his shirt over his mouth. Jumping off Majestic, he swiftly maneuvered along the threatening, smoke-filled air. In the distance, he heard the crackle of the fire and knew his time to find Jake was running short. He bumped into something solid. Jake lay motionless on the trail.

He stooped. "Jake." No response. Trent swung Jake's right arm over and across his back, lifting the old man to an upright position.

Jake coughed.

"Jake." Trent earned a raspy groan. "Jake, stay with me. We're getting out of here." He hefted him onto the horse, draped over resting on his stomach, and mounted behind him.

"Let's get a move on, Majestic," he said, taking the reins. Anxiety passed, and urgency kicked his adrenaline into high gear.

The closer they got to the fields, the less dense the smoke became. He heard the sirens of the fire trucks.

He picked up the pace in the clearing and spotted an ambulance by the barns. The EMTs took Jake off the horse and onto a stretcher, while Trent filled them in on where and how he found the older man. One EMT checked Trent and handed him an oxygen mask. They made him use it when he pushed it away.

"Is he okay?" he asked, lifting the mask off his face.

"Pulse is weak. Thready. He's inhaled a lot of smoke. We need to get him to the hospital."

Assured the fire department had the fire under control, he demanded, "I'm going along." Receiving no objection, he jumped in after they loaded Jake into the ambulance.

~ * ~

Maggie walked into the house and immediately smelled her father's cologne. "Daddy?" she called. She met him in the hall where they embraced each other in a long hug.

"Honey, it's good to see you." He held her within arm's reach. "Let me get a good look at my girl."

"Mom wasn't sure you'd be stopping, but I'm glad you could."

"I've missed my girl and wanted to pay a visit to see where I'm boarding her horse." He peered at his watch. "Let me take you to dinner, and we can catch up."

"I've missed you and Mom." She hugged her father again.

"We've missed you, too. Let's go to the Daiquiri Deck. I could go for a good burger and a cold beer. And I know how you love those daiquiris."

Maggie appreciated that her father would go to the Daiquiri Deck. The very casual atmosphere, patio style tables and open air didn't turn him away. Her mother was another story. She wouldn't be caught dead in the place.

Seated on the patio, she ordered a Green Parrot and a Grilled Chicken Club Wrap. Steven ordered a beer and the Deck Burger.

Their drinks arrived, and she relaxed until her father asked, "So, are you dating anyone? Your mother may have mentioned something to me about you seeing a gentleman."

"Daddy," she scolded and hoped she wasn't blushing as she twisted a section of hair.

"It's a legitimate question. So?"

Her face grew warm and not because of the heat. "Yes, there is someone I'm seeing." She shifted in her chair.

"Will I get to meet this man?" he asked with a smile.

"Yes."

Not ready to reveal Trent's name, she talked about him without mentioning it. "He's tall with dark hair, likes horses, races boats, and works hard at his job." She kept things very brief and noted her father smiled the entire time she talked. Could he be that happy she was dating again?

"You don't have to work tomorrow, do you?"

"No. What would you like to do?"

"Would you like to play eighteen rounds of golf?"

"No, you know golf was never my sport." She chuckled at the thought of her last round with her father. After losing two of his best balls, he'd given her some less expensive ones to use. She'd ended up losing four of those.

"We could ride horses. They rent horses for riding at Rolling Rock Ranch, don't they?"

"Yes, they do. We can call in the morning to see if they have something available." She squirmed in her seat.

"Sounds good, sweetheart."

They returned to the house, and Maggie checked for messages. Thank God, none were from Kevin, but Trent had left a jumbled one. Something about a fire, being at the hospital and would try her later. Why didn't he call her cell phone?

"What's wrong, Maggie?" Her father could see worry on her face, concern mixed with confusion.

"Nothing. Just a weird message." She couldn't tell him what it was about because it involved Trent and would reveal who he was in her life.

"You seem troubled."

"It was a jumbled message from Chloe. I'll call her back later."

"Okay. If you don't mind, it's been a long day, and I'd like to get some sleep. Glad you could accommodate your old man here," he grinned.

She gave him a hug. "I'm glad you're here, too. See you in the morning."

She went to her room and located the portable phone. While waiting for Trent to call her back and make some sense out of his message, she got ready for bed. She sat on her sofa and read a book to pass time. The phone rang.

It could be Kevin.

"Hello," she answered with reserve.

"I'm glad you're home."

"Trent, what's going on? Are you okay?"

"I'm fine, but Jake's spending the night at the hospital for smoke inhalation."

"What?" she exclaimed.

"There was a fire at the ranch on one of the riding trails. Jake got caught on the trail, and I found him. He'll be okay, but they're investigating the cause of the fire."

Kevin. But why? What did she do? She honestly couldn't think of what she had done to make him act on his threat. "Is there a lot of damage?"

"We're lucky there wasn't a strong wind. The fire burned slowly with everything so green and little brush to help fuel the fire. There was a lot of smoke though."

"I'm glad everyone is okay. When you see Jake..." Choked up, she couldn't continue.

"I'll let him know. I need to go. I'll talk to you later."

"Good night," Maggie hung up and cried. What did she do to make Kevin do this? She knew he was involved. At least Jake was okay.

Disturbed by Trent's call, when the phone rang she answered without thinking.

"You need to stay away from the pharmacy and keep a low profile at the hospital."

"Kevin?" She began to cry.

"I don't want to hurt anyone else."

"Why? I was seeing what my options were."

"I'm not fooling around. Now you know. I'll be calling for your decision on the matter–soon."

Chapter Nineteen

"Honey, are you ready?" her father called. "We need to get a move on. Our reservations are for seven."

They were dining at the Columbia. A casual to formal restaurant, but most people dressed up for dinner. Her parents had taken her to dinner at the Columbia several times when she joined them on vacation.

"Just a minute," she shouted. "Doing the finishing touches."

Two men held a conversation when she came down the stairs, which she found odd. She stepped around the corner into the kitchen, and the talking immediately stopped. Both sets of eyes gazed at her, but her mouth dropped open.

"Trent?" she mouthed in disbelief.

"Maggie, I'd like you to meet my good friend, but then again, I think you two already know each other," Steven said as he hugged her.

"What the hell? What's going on here?" The two men glanced at each other. "Well?" she asked, nervous and unsure of the situation.

"I called Trent and told him I'd be coming to pay a visit to see where I'm boarding your horse. And surprise my daughter with a visit."

"What did Trent tell you?" She turned to him and glared into his eyes, signaling he'd better not have said anything.

"Not much. That's why I inquired at dinner last night."

"Were you surprised to see your father?" Trent asked, walking to Maggie's side. He slid his arm around her waist, but not without her giving him the evil eye.

"Very." She turned to her father and said, "You should've gone with me this morning to the ranch. Then you could've seen where Blue is staying."

"Already have. That's why I made plans to go golfing with an old friend."

"You've already seen the ranch?"

"Yesterday. It's a beautiful place. I understand why you miss home. Now let's go have a nice dinner."

She wore a fitted red silk spaghetti strapped dress with red, strappy, high-heeled sandals. She opted to pull the hair off her neck, piled on top of her head. It was a tough decision to make, since this put the scar within plain view. She used the special makeup her mother had insisted on buying, which helped with the comfort level of having her hair up.

"You're beautiful," Trent whispered in her ear.

"Thank you," she stated, gliding toward the door. She stepped outside, pleased with Trent's reaction.

~ * ~

Dinner started with a positive note until Maggie spotted Kevin alone at a table near the patio. The genuine laughter shared during earlier conversation grew forced because of his presence. He sat watching her, and she struggled to stay focused.

Relief came as their table was cleared of plates and knowing they could leave soon. She remembered the disturbing phone call from Kevin and asked Trent, "How's Jake doing?"

"He's doing well and will be going home tonight. I told him to take a couple days off or more if he needs it."

"What are you two talking about?"

"There was a fire at the ranch after you left." Trent said, and Maggie nodded for him to tell. "My foreman got caught in the smoke and is in the hospital. The fire department is investigating. I'm convinced it was arson and not the weather."

Maggie glanced to where Kevin sat. He had the audacity to raise his glass to her. She gave the men at her table her attention.

"Glad to hear they're investigating."

"The trail has been closed. I'm hoping to have some answers in the coming week, but so far they're not saying much."

Maggie sat close to Trent and wanted to tell him who did it, but knew Kevin wouldn't have set the fire himself. He had someone else do it for him. Nothing would be traced back to him. The police had never connected Kevin to the incident with Mike, so Maggie doubted they would be able to with the fire.

A chair slid across the tiled floor in the Columbia Restaurant. Maggie turned in Kevin's direction, wide-eyed. Her stomach churned as panic nudged relief aside.

He approached their table. "Maggie, I hope the flowers I've sent have helped with your decision process. I also thought they'd brighten your home."

"Actually," she said as Trent placed his hand over hers, "they did brighten up the house, but I can't say I've made a choice." The smile on her face was a façade.

"I look forward to hearing from you on what you decide." Kevin extended his hand to her father. "Kevin Shaw."

"Steven Carlisle, Maggie's father. What decision does she have to make?"

"He sells home security systems." She addressed her father and glanced at Trent, who squeezed her hand. Her gaze returned to Kevin. "I haven't decided yet, so he's waiting for my answer which I'll have by this weekend." The cordial smile on her face diminished.

Kevin continued to hold eye contact with her and then glanced around the table at everyone. "I don't want to keep you from dinner. Mr. Carlisle, it was a pleasure to meet you." He extended his hand and then nodded at Trent, stating, "Good luck at the race next weekend."

"Are you going?" Trent asked as he continued to hold Maggie's hand affectionately.

"No, I don't have plans to," Kevin said, his gaze landing back on Maggie. "We'll talk soon."

"I'll be in touch," she said with an affable smile.

Kevin sauntered away while Maggie held a little tighter to Trent's hand. So as not to give any signs of distress to her father, Maggie ordered dessert instead of insisting on going home.

~ * ~

As they drove home from the restaurant Steven asked, "Sweetheart, you seemed uncomfortable with Kevin around. Has he done or said something inappropriate?"

"No. We did go for drinks once. I think he's having a difficult time with me dating Trent."

Trent held Maggie's hand in his.

"Well, if he becomes a nuisance, you let Trent know. If it gets worse, call the police. I don't want to see you in trouble again."

"I know, Daddy. Trent's taking good care of me." She squeezed his hand.

He leaned over and delivered a light kiss on her cheek above the scar line. She quickly pulled away. It was obvious she still wasn't comfortable with him being close to her scar.

When they'd parked in the driveway, Maggie started inside, but he took her by the hand. "Don't I get a good night kiss?"

"Sorry, I'm a little distracted."

"Come here." He pulled her into his arms. "Let me take everything away." At first the kiss was warm, he relished the taste of her lips and then deepened the kiss for the full flavor. She relaxed into him and shared in his enjoyment. His words brushed warm against her mouth. "Now, I want you to get a good night of sleep because Blue and I will be expecting you tomorrow morning."

"Thanks, I needed that." She delivered one quick kiss before letting him go.

Trent wished he could stay the night and hold her until morning. But he was courting Ms. Carlisle, and it wouldn't be appropriate with her father staying at the beach house.

The ordeal with Kevin resulted in straining their relationship and added stress to Maggie's life that she didn't need. It took a lot of will power at dinner not to stand up and confront Kevin right in the restaurant. Trent had been amazed at Maggie's strength and quick-witted thinking during the conversation they'd shared.

He had spent some time thinking about what they could do to get her out of the situation. But not being able to go to the police made it challenging. He would have to think about bringing the subject up to Steven. Maybe he'd have an idea or solution to the problem.

~ * ~

Maggie pulled to a stop at the front of the ranch, and Trent greeted her with a hug and kiss. "Are you ready for some fun? I think Blue's excited to see you."

"You've seen her already?" She pulled back from the embrace.

"I went to her last night after I got home from dinner. I missed you and thought maybe she could help."

"Did she?"

"Not much." He gave her a kiss. "Why don't we go to the barn and get the horses ready before I carry you into the house and take *you* for a ride instead."

"Blue first. You'll come later." She gave him a teasing slap on the chest.

"Oh, I hope so."

It dawned on her what she had said and gave him another slap on the chest. They strolled toward the stables.

~ * ~

"Which trail?" she asked from atop her mount. A slight breeze blew from the south and warmed the already balmy air. It was a beautiful day for a ride, swimming, and dinner outdoors.

"I'll lead the way." He trotted down the path and into the woods. "We'll stop here." He halted Majestic in a small clearing.

She dismounted and wondered what they'd stopped for. Trent pulled a blanket from one of the sidesaddle bags and then from the other side pulled out a small picnic basket.

"What's this?"

"I thought we could enjoy a little picnic lunch and have some private time before your father gets here."

"So, what do you have inside that basket of yours?" She helped spread the blanket out.

"Some crackers and cheese, fruit, and a little wine. Are you interested?"

"Actually," she stepped closer to him, "I want something else." She pulled him flush against her chest and teased his lips with her tongue before kissing him.

He broke the kiss and said tenderly into her ear, "Maggie, I want to have you here at my special place." He captured her lips with his own, eager to have her.

She tugged his shirt from his pants and pulled it over his head. He undid the buttons of her tank top while softly kissing her exposed skin. Goose bumps covered her, despite the ninety-six-degree heat.

"You always smell so sweet," he murmured.

Lips and tongue worked the delicate skin around her nipple, sending a new wave of goose bumps over her. He kissed to her navel where he pulled off her pants. Leisurely kissing his way back to her warm delicious mouth, he took it feverishly and held her warm body against him. His hand slid across her stomach, then lowered it, making her arch and gasp. She murmured his name as he teased her body and took her to the edge.

"Relax. Let it go," he said as she tensed.

"Now," she said breathlessly. "I need you now."

Trent took possession of her mouth as she divested him of his jeans. He finished getting them off the remainder of the way and during the process, took the condom from his back pocket. She found him ready with the condom on and nearly came at the feel of his entry.

Slowly they made love. He rolled to his back, letting her take control. It wasn't long before she came, and he followed soon after.

"I love you, Maggie Carlisle."

She lay there still and quiet. How could the words come so easily for him? Maybe he said it because he thought she needed to hear it. Several minutes passed before she broke the silence.

"Trent, I can't...I mean there's too much going on. Having gone through a divorce, moving away from my home and starting a new job and now Kevin's brought back the past... I can't," she trailed off, "I'm unsure of my feelings," she said softly and with great reluctance. "All I can say is...I love the time I spend with you."

"Maggie, you make it sound as if you're leaving—or I might be. I'm not going anywhere. And as far as Kevin's concerned, I'm going to help you." He paused. "As much as I would like to hear you say the words, I don't want you to say them until you mean them."

He tenderly kissed her lips. "I want you to know how much I love you, and that's why I'm telling you. I don't want to express my love with sex, although I do enjoy showing you." He wiggled his eyebrows at her. "I feel it's important to hear the words." He kissed her again. "I love you, Maggie, and you'll say it when you're ready."

She seized his mouth with want and when her hand took the length of him, he became aroused. "Make love to me," she whispered. "Again."

He slowed the pace, flipped her onto her back and took his time. After he came, he collapsed on top of her, but immediately slid to the side and murmured words of love.

She got dressed while Trent unloaded the spread of food from the basket. The sweet scent of fresh strawberries and the tang of pineapple teased her senses. He also had fresh melons and grapes.

"You packed an awful lot of food for two people," she commented.

"I thought we might need it after our ride."

"Which one?" She sat down on the blanket next to him and kissed him teasingly.

"Mmm, no comment."

"Sure, plead the fifth."

"Like I said, no comment. I'm famished. Let's eat."

Chapter Twenty

"The water is very comfortable," Steven said, pulling himself out of the pool as Trent and Maggie strolled up from the stables.

"Glad you made yourself at home before we got back," Trent said, standing next to Maggie.

"I'm going in to change." Maggie went into the house and thought about what Trent had said about love and Kevin. So far, he hadn't come up with a plan, and the call would come tomorrow morning.

With no answer for Kevin, and Trent telling her he loved her, things were very difficult. Her stomach betrayed her by fluttering at his words of love. Her heart nearly let the words slip from her mouth. She had quickly swallowed them.

She didn't want to steal drugs for Kevin. It went against her morals and beliefs. But how could she date a man who did these things? *Date* wasn't the word. Kevin wanted a permanent long-term relationship.

Could she live life within the façade? Could she walk away from Trent? What *were* her feelings towards him? Did she love him? Could it be possible, after this short a period? Trent was perfect, while she was marred by her past and no longer held the beauty she once did.

Her past would always haunt her if she had a personal relationship with Kevin. He would remind her every day of that past because he was a part of it.

She wiped away the tears rolling on her cheeks, took a few deep breaths, pulled herself together and went to join the men. Trent and her father stopped their conversation when she stepped outside.

154

Water dripped from Trent's swimsuit as he approached and greeted her with a kiss. "Everything okay? You were inside for some time."

"Fine. Guess it takes women a little longer to get dressed than men. What were you and my father talking about?" She worried he may have mentioned Kevin and the situation.

"Horses."

"Horses?" she asked in disbelief.

"Yes." He took her by the hand. "Don't worry. I didn't say anything."

Anything about us, Kevin or both, she questioned in silence.

They joined her father poolside and swam. At one point, Trent and her father got out of the pool, while she stayed behind to soak in more sun. She could hear their conversation about boat racing and relaxed enough to fall asleep.

Maggie opened her eyes at the gentle touch on her thigh. Trent sat on the edge of the pool next to her where the floating chaise had come to rest.

"Something's wrong, and I want to know what it is."

"Trent…"

"No, I want to know what's wrong. I can tell by the way you've distanced yourself."

"I'm afraid about tomorrow. We haven't thought of a plan, and he'll be calling. I'm scared. I don't like either of my options. And I don't want to think about what he'll do if I choose neither option."

"It'll be okay. Let's get ready for dinner." He kissed her forehead. "I love you."

~ * ~

Near the end of dinner, Trent glanced at Maggie and then to her father. "Maggie, I'm sorry. Steven, Mike's past…"

"Trent! No!" She stood with anger boiling in her veins. "How could you?"

He stood and took her hands. "Maggie, he has a right to know. You're his daughter, and he loves you. I love you, and he might be capable of helping you."

"Please, honey, sit back down. I want to hear what Trent has to say. Unless you'd rather tell me what's going on?"

She sat as both men peered at her with waiting eyes. "Kevin, the man you met last night, isn't selling me a security system." She pulled the usual section of hair forward and played with it. "He...he wants me to make a different decision."

"What kind of decision, and what does this have to do with Mike?" her father inquired.

"Mike worked with Kevin in the drug business...the illegal kind." She needed Trent's support, and he delivered when he took her hands in his. "He gave me two choices."

"And these two choices he's given you?" His voice was stern. "What are they?"

"Basically, it's him, or I become a supplier." She bowed her head in shame. Shame for getting herself into another mess. Shame for not standing up for herself. Shame for not being the one to tell her father.

"What?" Steven's voice rose in anger. "What do you mean it's him or you become a supplier?"

"Sir," Trent shifted his hand onto her leg. "He either wants Maggie to have a personal relationship with him, or she steals drugs he wants from the hospital, becoming his supplier."

"That's the most ridiculous thing I've ever heard of. How does he expect you to get them?"

Maggie couldn't glance at her father, knowing he would be staring at her. Trent's caress on her thigh was a slight help to keep her calm.

"She has access, but I think he knows she won't do it because of Mike. I'd bet he believes she'll decide to be with him instead."

"Why haven't you called the police?" her father asked.

"Supposedly, he has connections within the department. He said he would do other things, hurtful things, if she called," Trent informed him.

"I'd like to go home." She stepped away from the table.

Her father knew about everything, knew she was in trouble again. She didn't want help from anyone. This was supposed to be her time. Her time to grow and be on her own. Damned Kevin!

~ * ~

Maggie shuffled zombie-like into the house and to her room. She went out to the balcony and glanced to the ocean in hopes this saga would not continue like the expanse of water before her. The air was full of humidity, and she welcomed the slight breeze. A storm was brewing, and not just in the atmosphere.

The steps creaked. Knowing what was coming, she prepared to face her father.

"Daddy, I'm sorry I didn't call and tell you sooner, but I wanted to take care of this on my own."

He approached the railing where she stood. "It's okay, honey. I understand. When Trent initiated talk about Mike at dinner, I was shocked. Hurt at first, but you're a grown woman, and you have every right to want to do things on your own. But I'm here. I'm involved. And I'm going to help."

"Oh, Daddy." She went into his open arms.

"It'll be okay." He let her cry. "We'll take care of this awful situation with Kevin, and Mike will finally be out of your life. Trent should be here soon."

"Trent?" She backed out of his arms.

"We need a plan. I talked with your mother."

"You talked to Mom? She knows?" She didn't think her stomach could sink any lower, but it did and became a tumultuous storm of bile.

"Yes," he said simply. "She made a suggestion I think might work. But I want to talk about it with Trent and you." He peered at her, and added, "Plus, I think you'll need him tonight and throughout the day tomorrow."

"But—"

"No buts about it. You're going to need him. I'm okay with the boy staying here. He should be here when Kevin calls." He stepped into the bedroom and said, "I need to get downstairs and start making a few calls."

Maggie sat outside. Would her mother tell the family about the situation? What idea could her mom have come up with? What was her father thinking of for a plan? And Trent? What was her father doing, inviting him to come to the house? Her mind spun out of control like a spin art wheel. Then Kevin crept in.

What was she going to do? She knew she couldn't get away with stealing drugs from the hospital. They were already watching her. Her only other option was to—she simply couldn't think about it.

Relieved to have help from Trent and her father, she couldn't depend on them and them alone. She needed to stand up for herself and see if she could come up with a possible resolution. So far, the only one she saw possible was to agree to be with *him*.

"Maggie, can you please come down here? We need to talk about tomorrow." Her father called up to her from the bottom of the stairs.

There he stood, waiting with open arms at the bottom of the stairs, and she went into them. Trent pulled her in tight with a hug, kissed the top of her head and walked with her to the living room.

She sat in the floral chair, and Trent sat on the arm next to her.

"I've called a friend on the hospital board to see what possibilities we may have, asking the hospital to work with us. But as our first option, I'm calling the DEA and Mike. Kevin never mentioned going to a higher authority. He sounds like a good catch for the Feds."

She didn't say a word when her father mentioned Mike's name. He couldn't leave the state of Texas per his bail bond agreement, and therefore, wouldn't be coming to Florida anytime soon.

"Do you think calling Mike is a good idea?" Trent asked as he caressed her hand.

"Yes. He knows Kevin, and maybe he'll know how to get to him."

"What is Maggie going to tell Kevin?" Trent asked.

"Maggie, I want you to tell him you'll be his supplier. We'll figure the rest after that. I'll be making more calls tomorrow, so hopefully I'll know more then." He glanced at her. "Maggie, did you hear me?"

"Yes. But I don't want to talk to Mike." There was no feeling. She wasn't angry or sad or remorseful. She just knew she didn't want to talk to him.

"You won't have to. I will. You take care of Kevin by telling him you'll get his drugs."

"I'd like to go to bed now," she said in a catatonic voice.

"Go ahead, honey. I'll see you in the morning." Steven said to Trent, "Go take care of her. She needs you more than ever."

The lights were off, and clouds covered the light of the moon when Trent approached her on the balcony. Softly he called her name. She turned and stared into his eyes.

He pulled her into his arms. "It's going to be okay, Maggie. Everything is going to be okay." Kissing the top of her head, he held her and didn't say another word.

Sprinkles fell as lightning and thunder played on the horizon. They walked back into the room, and she closed the patio door, leaving the window coverings open.

He held her on the small sofa for a short time. "I think we should move to the bed and go to sleep."

Maggie said nothing as she went into the bathroom where she put on her pajamas and brushed her teeth. He set his overnight kit on the counter and brushed his teeth. She left the room, asleep on her feet.

Under the covers, he held her tense body against his and wished she would relax and ease into a deep sleep. He told himself he wouldn't fall asleep first, so he fought it until he felt her relax in his arms.

~ * ~

Maggie awoke to a flash of lightning followed by a loud clap of thunder. Cautious not to wake Trent, she slid from the bed and sat on the sofa, watching the storm through the patio doors.

She figured she hadn't been asleep for long because the storm should have passed quicker, as they usually did on the shore. The red glowing lights on her clock read past two in the morning. She had slept three hours. Another storm must've rolled through.

Morning would soon be approaching, and she re-thought the plan. Like her father said, she was an adult. This was her time to step up and face the reality of the situation. She rehashed some of her own thoughts and ideas and when she felt better about what the morning would bring, she snuggled back into Trent's arms. The storm passed, and the night was quiet once more.

"Where are you going?" he asked sleepily at her movement.

"Nowhere. I—" She thought about what to say. "Getting a little more comfortable." She ran her hand over his chest and down the trail of hair. "Make love to me."

"Maggie, your father's downstairs. I already feel bad enough I'm in your bed when we're not married."

"I think it's obvious he likes and approves of you." She paused briefly and gazed into his eyes with pain and desire. "Trent, I need you to make love to me."

"Are they still...?"

She nodded her head, answering his unfinished question about the condoms, and kissed his chest as he reached for the drawer. There would be nothing quick about this round between the sheets.

She'd found love for the last time.

Maggie cried herself to sleep, knowing what lay ahead. Tomorrow she would protect Trent, the ranch, Team Seahorse and her family. Tonight, she made love to him with her heart and soul. It hurt to her core to know it would be the last time she would be with him.

Chapter Twenty-One

Maggie woke to her father's booming voice and the smell of bacon. She sat against her pillows and glanced at the time. Eight o'clock loomed, and her body wanted to stay put instead of taking a shower. She headed downstairs wrapped in her robe.

She rounded the corner to the kitchen and heard her father. "So, how did you both sleep?" She paused to hear Trent's response.

"As well as expected. I don't think she got much rest, and she looks like hell," he snarled. "I could kill the bastard, but I refuse to lay a hand on him for her sake. I can't wait for this to be done with."

"I couldn't agree more."

"Well," she came around the corner, "it will be done within an hour or so." She poured a cup of coffee and went to her favorite flowered chair, although the flowers were not cheering her up today. Her stomach wavered like a violent ocean.

"Honey, come eat," Steven said.

"I'm not hungry, but thanks." She couldn't trust her stomach to keep anything down.

"Maggie Marie Carlisle, you come to this table and eat this breakfast I've fixed for you. After all, I am still your father."

It had been many years since she heard her dad raise his voice using her full name, and she knew better than to go against him. She smiled at her father while sitting down to scrambled eggs, toast, and bacon.

"Thank you. I'm just unsure of how it will settle." There was a small glass of orange juice, too.

Steven set a plate on the counter in front of Trent who asked, "What about you? Aren't you going to eat?"

"I was up early and ate," Steven answered, cleaning the fry pan.

Halfway through eating the phone rang. Nine o'clock on the dot. Maggie glanced at Trent, then at her father. Her heart pounded against her tightening chest. She swore it would break through or stop from the pressure.

Light headed and shaking, she picked up the phone that sat on the counter. The plan had played repeatedly inside her head all night long.

"Good morning, Maggie. Do you have my answer?" Kevin's smooth talking sent chills down her spine.

"Yes."

"And what have you decided?"

She slid off the breakfast barstool and moved through the living room as the two men stared at her. At the patio door, she stepped onto the deck and over to the rail.

"Maggie?" Kevin inquired.

She took a deep breath and replied with a quick exhale, "I'm here." Turning at the sound of Trent and her father coming onto the deck, Maggie rotated back to face the Gulf. "I need to see you."

"You only need to tell me what your answer is. You've had long enough to decide."

Her skin prickled, and hair stood up on the back of her neck. He's a cold one all right.

"I need to see you before I make my final decision." She would not and could not let this request go.

"Meet me in a half hour at the White Sand Public Beach Pavilion. *Alone.*"

"I'll be there." She heard the dial tone. Now came the toughest part.

"What the hell do you think you're doing? We already made a decision. What do you need to meet him for?" Trent barked.

"I know what I'm doing," Maggie shouted back at him. He had every right to be angry, but she had to stay firm. "I'm a grown woman, and I'm making the decision on my own terms." She stormed into the house and headed for her room.

"Maggie." He caught up with her and seized her arm. "I love you. I just don't want to see you get hurt."

"Please let go. You're hurting me." She used her anger to fight. The pit of her stomach knotted, and tears stung her eyes with sadness.

"I'm sorry." He released her arm.

Maggie continued to her room. She showered, leaving enough time to be alone before she met Kevin.

Trent and her father sat in the living room talking when she came downstairs. She took in a deep breath and exhaled, to calm her already frazzled nerves and walked to the patio door.

"Don't go, Maggie. Don't go against our plans," Trent said, taking her hand.

"What plans? So far, all you want me to do is tell him I'll get the drugs. That isn't a plan." She pulled her hand from his. "What happens when I can't get him the drugs he wants? I'll tell you. He sends someone after me. Do you see this?" She turned and jutted her jaw, exposing the scar. "This is what happens when you don't make good on the deal. I need to go now." Her decision made last night, she had to stand firm and follow through.

"Do what you need to then. Remember," he pulled her close and planted a firm kiss on her lips, "I love you."

She walked barefoot to the beach. Today when her bare feet touched the sand, invisible shards of glass pricked at her feet and heightened every nerve in her body. Gone—the magical calming effect of the cool soft sand—gone.

She made her way to the beach pavilion, mentally going over her questions. Her father mentioned calling the DEA and Mike, but nothing further had been mentioned regarding them in the matter of Kevin. Their plan was no plan at all other than to lie to the man and risk everyone around her being hurt.

With no sign of Kevin upon her arrival, she sat at one of the tables. Her stomach quavered. Nerves tingled and twitched. She watched the waves crash and caress the sandy shoreline. The ocean didn't quell her body's heightened awareness of the conversation about to take place.

"Maggie." He crept up behind her. She startled, and her body hiccupped on the bench.

"Let's walk along the shore," Maggie said as she stood up.

"Why did we need to meet?" He followed behind her until they hit the sand, where he stepped beside her.

She took a deep breath and for a moment remained quiet. "I've made my decision, but before I finalize it, I need to set some ground rules." The words escaped her lips faster than anticipated. So much for deep breathing to calm the nerves.

"Go on. You've got my interest piqued."

"Will the relationship be sexual?"

He stopped walking, and without seeing his face, she knew he wore a dumbass grin. He walked around and stared directly at her. "In time, yes. Yes, I expect it to be sexual."

"How much time?" She strolled along again, clasping her hands together. Tightly.

"I'm not sure. I hope within a few weeks you'll see how loving I can be." He reached to touch her cheek, but she backed away. He returned his hand to his pocket. "We'll have to wait and see."

"And if by the time you expect it and I'm not ready, will you respect my decision?"

"I can't answer that."

Her stomach twisted at his response, and breakfast began to back up. She swallowed. Hard.

"These are my ground rules. I will continue to work at the hospital and *will not* do anything to risk my job. If you do anything to jeopardize it, I will *immediately* end this relationship. I will not move out of my house and into yours, and *you* will not move into mine. I will end my relationship with Trent, but will continue to go riding at his ranch."

Kevin started to interrupt, but she didn't allow it. Her tongue was like that of an auctioneer's. "You know my horse is being boarded at his ranch. I *will not* move her elsewhere. You are not permitted to go with me. You'll have to trust I will not be with Trent.

"I do not do drugs. If I find you've slipped me *anything* or try to pressure me in *any way*, again, I will end this relationship."

Maggie stopped, as did Kevin. She glared at him. As frigid as the ice-cold waters of the Arctic Ocean, she said, "I do not *like* you, nor do I approve of your lifestyle, but you have left me with no other choice. If you agree to my rules, then you know my decision. If you are unable to agree to my rules, then I will need to work on the other option. So, what is it?" Her heart hammered against her chest, and her ears roared.

"I can and will, for a period of time, work with your rules. I'm pleased...but surprised by your choice."

"So am I."

"Now, for *my* rules," the words rolled off his tongue slow and steady.

Her skin prickled, and a lump formed in her throat.

"If I find out you are with Randall in any way, other than visiting your horse, I'll take matters into my own hands to rid us of the problem. Whether it be Randall, your horse, or the whole ranch—who knows?"

"If you—"

He cut her off as she'd done to him. The trapdoor to her stomach opened, and the bile began its ascent.

"If you jeopardize *my* 'business' in any way, well, I'm not sure what my course of action will be. I'm not out to hurt you. You'll find I can give you the lifestyle you deserve. The lifestyle Mike couldn't give you. The lifestyle Randall isn't worthy of giving you. I will make you happy, Maggie." He reached to take her hand, but she denied him the satisfaction. "You'll see. You have through Friday to end things between you and Trent."

She swallowed several times to kick the bile back to its rightful place. "How kind of you," she sneered.

"Have a great week, beautiful," he said sauntering away, leaving her standing there.

Now came the hardest part of this whole ordeal. She strolled back to the house. Did she make the right decision? Yes. She had done the right thing. She wouldn't be able to live with herself if she stole drugs from the hospital, or if something happened to her family, Trent or anyone else.

The men sat on the deck. Trent spotted her and ran down the steps as she approached the house.

"Maggie, you're okay," he said, joining her in the sand.

Be firm. Be strong. Her palms clammy, she patted them on her shorts as though that would make them better. Her heart raced like a herd of wild horses on the open prairie. "Of course I'm okay. I took care of things." Her stomach churned, and her eyes burned, wanting to release the tears. She wasn't okay.

"What the hell happened?" He raised his voice.

"The situation has been handled. I made my own decision." Her voice quavered as she continued to walk toward the deck.

"What the hell does that mean? Tell me you didn't go against the plan." His eyes darted wildly.

"I think maybe it's time for you to leave." She held strong, and the quiver in her voice dissipated.

"What?" Trent was downright pissed. He stopped at the base of the steps.

"You heard me." She stepped past him to go up the stairs.

"What the hell did you do, Maggie?" When she didn't answer, he yelled, "You told him you would be with him." He took a firm hold of her arm. "Didn't you?"

She yanked her arm from his grip, raised her voice to meet his and said determinedly going up the stairs, "It was *my* choice, and *I* made it."

At this point, they had gained the attention of the few people on the beach.

On the deck, she passed her father and said, "I'm leaving, and when I get back I want him out of here." Entering the house, she snatched her keys and purse, went to the garage and left.

~ * ~

Trent stood in a state of shock. Steven studied the patio door where Maggie had disappeared then glanced back to Trent. Neither of them could believe what she had done.

"Where did I go wrong? I thought we had it planned?" Trent asked in disbelief. His heart shriveled at love lost, yet beat heavily in anger. "You heard her. She's going to be with that slime ball."

"I think you should go." Steven rested his hand on Trent's back and guided him inside. "I'm going to think this through and talk to her. I'll call you."

Trent didn't say anything as he went upstairs, but came back down a few minutes later. "I'm not leaving. I won't let her do this." His heart swelled, refilling its rightful spot.

"I'm not about to stop you. But be warned, she's not going to be happy."

"I'll deal with it, but I'm not leaving." Blood coursed through his veins in anticipation of facing Maggie again.

"She might get a little pushy, but I'm sure you can handle it. Glad you're not walking away so easily, but maybe you should go upstairs for a while. You know, stay out of the way."

"Okay, but I think we need to decide what to do."

The two men sat thinking, then Trent went to the kitchen and started digging around in the drawers.

"What are you searching for?" Steven asked curiously.

"She went on a few dates with him. She has his business card somewhere."

"What are you thinking?"

"Not sure. But having his number will be a plus for me." Trent headed upstairs.

A few minutes later Steven yelled up, "I think I found it."

Trent tromped down the stairs two at a time and took the card Steven held out to him. Luck was on their side. Scribbling the numbers onto a piece of paper, he handed the card back to Steven. "Put it back where you found it."

"I need to make a call. You'd better keep your eyes open for Maggie since you're supposed to be gone."

Trent nodded in agreement, and Steven left, pushing buttons on his cell phone.

~ * ~

A shattered heart lay in her chest cavity, and tears blurred her vision. Maggie pulled off to the side of the road, her body having taken over the controls. She didn't know where she was going and had driven for an hour. She shook and sobbed until her nose was a snotty mess.

She had to leave, knowing he would be angry and hurt. He loved her body and soul. His words came back to haunt her, 'I love you, Maggie, and you'll say it when you're ready.' A new explosion of tears spilled onto her cheeks as the uncontrollable shaking continued. What had she done?

What would Saturday bring when her new relationship with Kevin started? Would he expect to kiss her? She had only said sexual, and a kiss wasn't sexual in the sense she'd meant.

Whether Trent knew it or not, the first kiss between them *had been* sexual and had her burning hot to her core. Chills swept over her, and goose bumps formed. She rubbed her arms to make the bumps go away, only they wouldn't.

Enough time had passed for Trent to pull his things together and leave. She wiped her eyes and nose and decided to return home.

~ * ~

Furious his truck remained parked in front of the house she slammed her palms on the steering wheel. "I warned him to leave, and he has the nerve to stay." Her blood boiled. "I made my choice. A choice which no longer allows him to be a part of my life. My choice." She pulled into the garage. Rage was preparing to tear down her wall of protection. "Time to get nasty."

Entering the house, she took the stairs by two. "Trent," she yelled.

"Maggie, give him a chance. Listen to him." Her father met her at the top of the stairs from the garage.

"Daddy, there's nothing the two of you can do. Where is he?" She nudged past him into the living room. "Trent!"

"Maggie."

She turned. Damn Trent for being so compassionate. She released the anger and raised her voice. "Don't Maggie me in that sweet loving tone. You know *damn* well it's over between us."

"No, it's not!" He raised his voice to compliment hers. "I love you, and I'm not going to let you do this."

"What part didn't you understand? I want you to leave. It's over, Trent. I'm with Kevin." Her voice cracked as she fought back tears and swallowed the frog stuck in her throat.

"*Bullshit!* You belong with me." He made an effort to take her hands and lower his voice. "We belong together. I *know* your heart knows this, so why not unlock it. Tell Kevin the deal is off." His eyes were dark and smoldering, sending a hot wave into her belly.

"No. It's over between *us*." Bringing her hands to his chest, she pushed him back with as much force as she could muster. He wobbled off balance, and she yelled, "Get out of my house!" She thought about pushing him again, making him fall, but decided against it.

"Maggie, don't—"

"I said get out! Now!" She stomped up the stairs to her room.

She sat on the small sofa. No longer able to fight the tears, the floodgate opened, and she crumpled into the fetal position. She had to be tough to protect him. This was why she hadn't wanted him here when she got back. She'd wanted to avoid another confrontation and those damn blue eyes that touched her soul. She needed to regain her composure.

She drew a warm bath, lit candles, turned on the CD player and decided to soak away the day's pains. She wanted the day to come to an end, but had to go into work. She'd welcome the distraction work would bring.

The phone rang. She hoped her father would answer. Sure enough, the ringing stopped, and she eased back into the balmy lavender scented bath water and listened to Toni Braxton belt a song from her heart.

Chapter Twenty-Two

The moment the phone rang, he answered, "Good afternoon, Trent Randall," eager to hear good news from Steven. Yesterday had been a tough day for Maggie. He hoped within the next couple of days this whole Kevin situation would be finished.

"Trent, how are you?"

"I'm fine, Steven. How's Maggie?"

"She worked last night and is sleeping."

"She's still sleeping?" It was nearing three in the afternoon.

"Yeah, I think she took one of her pills."

"What kind of pill?" Trent raised his voice, both shocked and concerned.

"She has some prescription sleeping pills from the accident. I think after what happened she felt she needed one."

"Okay." The pill thing bothered him, but her father remained calm about it, so he let it go. "Anything new happening?"

"It's out of our hands, Trent. I do have to tell you, though, the DEA is *very* interested."

"Good. Maybe they'll get this taken care of quickly." There came a sense of relief, knowing Kevin would be out of their lives soon.

"We can only hope. You should know the DEA is bringing Mike to Florida to work for them on the case."

He knew there was more. "What's the plan, and does Maggie know Mike's coming to town?"

"No. Remember, we mentioned involving the DEA and Mike. She

met with Kevin before I heard back from the DEA. Now that we know they're taking control of the situation, I don't want to tell her anything else."

"I don't know, with Mike being here, and everything going on..."

"I plan on keeping it quiet. It's for her own good. The DEA is unable to tell me any details of their operation, so I don't want her getting her hopes up. I'll let you know if I hear anything though." Steven paused a moment. "Listen, I need to go. I think I hear her."

Trent sat in his office, wondering how things would play out. What did the DEA have planned? Would Maggie get hurt again? Was bringing Mike back into the picture a good idea? Maybe it wasn't such a bad plan. How else would they get to Kevin? He'd told her to walk away from Kevin and go to the authorities, but she had been unwilling. No, *stubborn* was the word.

He was happy and angry at the same time, thinking of the evening they spent together with her father. Kevin had ruined everything they had going, and she willingly threw it away.

"Jesus!" It slapped him in the face. "She never elaborated on the threats he made. He intimidated her using her family, the team and me as bait. I'd bet the ranch on it." He slammed his hands on top of the desk. Anger ran rampant through his veins.

"She deemed it necessary to protect me because she knows he had the damn fire set. She sacrificed her happiness to protect me. I'm going to go tell her to call Kevin and break off this whole deal. She doesn't need to protect the team or me."

And he didn't want to lose what they had together.

A knock sounded at his door, and Trent said tersely, "Come in."

"Sorry, but we need you at the boat barn." Chad paused before he asked, "Everything okay with you and Maggie? You sound a little upset."

Trent pushed his chair from the desk and walked through the door. "*No*, everything's not okay." He headed for the boat barn. "What she does with her time is her business, not mine. Why are you making such a big deal about this?"

"What happened? I thought you two were a couple?"

171

"What is it with you?" He stopped, glaring sternly at Chad, "You and Chloe got us together. Now we're apart. Maggie is a friend and business client." He continued to walk.

"That's bull, and you know it."

"And if it is," Trent turned around to face Chad, "it's none of your business." He spun back around and continued to the barn. "Maggie does what she wants in her own free time. Let it go."

"Gotcha, boss," Chad said, barely audible.

~ * ~

Maggie couldn't help but admire the dozen yellow roses she received from Trent while getting ready to leave for work Monday afternoon. She missed him but had made her decision and would stand behind it.

Once at work she had plenty to do to keep her busy, but was distracted by thoughts of Trent and Kevin. She answered the phone and hearing Kevin's voice on the other end shouldn't have surprised her, but it did. "What can I do for you?"

"Lighten up, Mags. You don't need to be professional with me. You're my girlfriend."

She clenched her teeth when he called her Mags and suppressed a scream at the mention of them being an item.

"I've made reservations for us Thursday night. I'll pick you up at six."

"Kevin, Thursday's not a good night."

"Thursday's going to be the perfect night, Mags. I'll see you at six."

He disconnected before she could protest further. Her father was leaving Wednesday and she wanted time for herself. The way he said it was going to be a perfect night sent dreadful shivers down her spine. He practically purred the words. She heard a light knock on the counter, jerking her in the chair while she still held the receiver.

"Maggie, are you okay?" A petite co-worker regarded her with a worried expression on her pixie face.

"Fine. A little tired, I guess. I'll be fine. I'm going to grab a cup of coffee. Do you want one?"

"As long as you're making the trip, why not. Thanks."

Maggie left the station and thought about the upcoming outing with Kevin. Would he expect her to stay out all night with dinner and dancing or would he keep it short, being Thursday evening? He didn't have the decency to tell her where they were going. She laughed at the thought of him dressing casual and visiting a place like Bob's Boat House.

Mentally she shook her head and refused to reflect on him or dinner. She would wait and see what Thursday brought.

~ * ~

Promptly at six, Kevin arrived. Maggie opened the door to find him with a dozen long-stemmed red roses.

"Thank you. I'll get a vase for these. Would you like a drink before we leave?"

"I have a business meeting at the restaurant before dinner. If you don't mind taking care of the flowers, I'd like to get going."

Maggie went to the kitchen, pulled a vase from the cupboard and carelessly, without water, tossed the roses in the container.

"I'm ready." She snatched her handbag off the ledge.

Kevin opened the car door and offered his hand to help her into her seat. She slid in without his assistance, yet he managed to run his hand along her back. She arched away then fidgeted with her purse and kept both hands on it the entire time.

The car smelled of men's cologne, and she crinkled her nose. A cool breeze from the air vents blew on her face, too much for her taste.

"Are you too cold? I can warm it up," he asked as she adjusted the vent direction.

"It'll be fine. It's blowing right in my face." The vent dealt with, she asked, "Where are we going?"

"Chinatsu Japanese Steak Restaurant."

"Oh." Not her first choice of places to go, but knowing Kevin, it would be a five-star restaurant.

He was quiet during the ride. She welcomed the silence, knowing that eventually they would have to talk.

"I'll find the person I'm meeting," he said, approaching the restaurant. "It shouldn't take long."

He parked and took her by the arm, which she accepted, and they entered the restaurant. Kevin led her into the bar. She couldn't believe who sat at the corner table in front of them.

Her ex-husband.

Maggie's mouth dropped open then quickly shut.

"Mike." Kevin stuck his hand out and shook Mike's. "Good to see you. Mags, I think you two know each other," he said smugly, pulling a chair out for her to sit in.

He sat beside her and placed his arm on the back of her chair. She sat straighter and despised him more than she thought possible. In a low growl, she struggled to control her temper and asked, "What the *hell* are you doing here? Isn't this a violation of your bail bond?"

"I'm having a meeting." Mike raised his voice. "What the hell are *you* doing with *him*?"

"I don't think that concerns you. We're divorced. Remember?" The growl disappeared, and her volume level rose.

"He's not what you need."

"I'll be the judge of that."

"Kevin," Mike turned away from her and lowered his voice. "tell me how you want to work this. I have a supply back at the hotel."

"You're feeling confident."

"You expressed interest, and I came through."

"What do you have, and how much?"

Mike leaned in toward Kevin and said in a whisper, "Ten mils of Dilaudid. It's a sample of what we can deliver for you."

"Sounds good for a start, but can you get more? Is your supplier willing to get other items I may want?"

"Yes, we can get more. Since I'm not working anymore, my friend has been slowly collecting over time and has a supply stashed away. You know it takes time, patience and skill with the hospital security. I can't say for other items, but I can get back to you during another delivery."

Maggie rolled her eyes every now and then, shaking her head in disbelief at what she was hearing. She didn't care what transpired between the two pieces of shit when they spoke too softly for her to hear what they were saying.

"Your supplier *is* eager for some extra dough. Why don't we wait and see how good this first batch is, then we'll go from there. Being as you have a nice supply for me, meet me at the marina at Marina Jack's. Slip twenty on the H-dock. You know where it is?"

"I'll find it. When? What time?"

"Saturday noon." Kevin stood with a smile, pulled Maggie's chair back and said, "Why don't you join us for dinner? It's been a while since we've talked."

"I don't think so," Mike replied, staying seated.

"Thank you," she said curtly and pushed her chair into the table. "Kevin and I are going to have a nice meal together before going back to my place."

"Maggie," Mike lowered his voice, "Don't do this. He's not the guy for you."

If she was going to make a scene, it had better be a good one. Throwing her hands on the table, she raised her voice, "What the hell do you know?" She hunched over the table, leaning toward him. "Like *you* were the guy for me? We both know what happened, and now it's over," She left the bar for the hostess stand.

"Kevin, I'll see you at noon Saturday," Mike said.

Kevin joined her, and they were seated at their table. With drinks ordered and delivered, she turned to Kevin who beamed with satisfaction. Taking a drink of wine, then with the same low growl used with Mike, she glared at Kevin and said, "Don't say anything. You did this to flaunt me in front of him because I'm with you. Well, you have me only because of, let's just say, false pretenses." Maggie finished off her wine and added, "And don't tell me you're sorry when you're not."

The wine, she hoped, would put her in a relaxed state. Seeing Mike was too much. She wanted another glass.

Kevin picked up his menu and gazed around the restaurant at the other patrons. "Why don't we order?"

She let him off easy this time, having had enough drama for the night. Unfortunately, as she sipped on a fresh glass of wine while waiting for their meal, she spotted Trent and fumed. First Mike and now Trent? Couldn't she have a quiet dinner? Not what she wanted with Kevin, but she didn't like these two other men interrupting, especially Trent. He knew she had made a choice, and it didn't include him.

"Excuse me," Maggie slid her chair back, "but there's someone I need to speak to." The man had a surprise coming, because she was in rare form and ready to fight.

"I'll be right here waiting, babe."

She left the table for Trent's, the word *babe* only fueling the fire more.

Firmly slamming her hands on Trent's table, enough to shake and spill his water, Maggie stared directly into his eyes and through clenched teeth said, "What are you doing here?"

"Can't a man eat?"

"That's bullshit, and you know it!" Instead of calming her, the wine had done the opposite. "You're checking up on me. Try another excuse."

"Maggie, I'm here having dinner."

"Trent, either you leave now, or I'll...I'll pull Blue Bonnet out of your stables." He touched her hand, but she pulled away and stood straight.

"So, what is it? Are you leaving or is Blue?"

He stood and stepped as close as she would permit. "I love you, Maggie. You've been drinking."

"What about it?"

"Wait before you do anything with him." Before she could say anything, he turned and left.

Kevin wore a large stupid grin on his face as she approached the table. The asshole was loving every minute of the evening.

"Wipe the grin off your face, or I'll do it for you," she said quietly and sat in her chair.

He reached for her hand, but she yanked it away. "Don't touch me," she hissed.

"Mags, I'll admit I knew Mike would be here, but I knew nothing about Trent. Personally, I'm pleased to see you telling him to get lost."

"Let's just get dinner over with." She took a steady sip of wine. It was her second, and would be, her final glass for the night. As Trent mentioned, she didn't need the alcohol to muddle up her thought process when it came to Kevin. The last thing she wanted to do was sleep with the low life.

They left the restaurant, and, once in his car, he suggested. "Why don't we hit one of the night clubs? The night is still young."

"I'm exhausted, and I've had enough for one night." It wasn't far from the truth. Her head felt like someone was drilling a tunnel at the lower base of her occipital bone, and the pain spread from there.

"You're right." He headed in the direction of her house. "You did have an eventful evening, seeing your ex-husband and your most recent ex in one evening."

"Eventful to say the least." Snide little bastard. Lying, she added, "I also have to work tomorrow and need my sleep."

"You work tomorrow?" His eyes furrowed as he glanced in her direction. "Your schedule doesn't show it."

"How do you know—my schedule?" Maggie squirmed in her seat. "Never mind, no need to answer. You have your ways."

He pulled into her driveway and turned off the purring engine.

"You don't need to walk me to the door."

"I hoped I could have the drink you offered earlier." His hand rested on her thigh.

"Kevin, like I said earlier, I'm very tired and would like to go to bed." Quickly adding, "Alone, Kevin. I'm going to bed alone, and you're not welcome inside." She opened the car door, and he grabbed her arm. She gasped, as concern for her safety grew.

"Mags, I'd like a kiss before you leave."

What a pretentious bastard. "Kevin, after what happened tonight and you being a part of it," she strived to remove her arm, "I don't think I could bring myself to do that right now." She glanced at her arm and then into his eyes. Anxiety and a sense of urgency settled around her like a dark storm cloud. She needed to get out of the car.

"Tonight, I'll let you go. But next time...I'll be expecting something more."

Released from his hold, she slammed the door of his precious Jaguar. The car's headlights illuminated the garage. She entered her code and disappeared behind the closing door before he backed away.

Entering the dark quiet house an immediate loneliness settled upon her. Her father had left yesterday morning. She leaned against the door and thought about the evening. Seeing Trent was one thing, Mike another. It was against court ruling for him to leave the state of Texas, and she hadn't expected to see him. It could mean only one thing if he met with Kevin. Mike was back in the game.

The red roses sat on the kitchen counter, looking like a red flag to a bull. Maggie snatched them up and threw them away. She didn't want anything from Kevin in the house. Unlike the yellow roses from Trent that sat on her dresser.

Upstairs, she sat on the edge of her bed and swallowed a pill. Ever since Kevin had entered the picture, she had taken the sleeping aids more than she liked.

With Kevin a part of her life, she didn't care if she became addicted to them. She needed something to put her mind at ease and give her a good night's sleep. With no work tomorrow, the drugs would do exactly that for her—put her out until sometime later.

Chapter Twenty-Three

Trent didn't feel like eating, but when Blanca fixed him a sandwich for lunch Friday, he figured he had better eat, or he would hear about it. His appetite had dropped considerably since Maggie left him.

Nearly a week had passed since their break up, and it not only affected his appetite, but he lacked sleep and didn't enjoy riding. Knowing she was protecting him and the crew, he had called her several times during the week to confront her about his suspicions. His calls went unanswered. She was ignoring, and avoiding him. He had become restless with work and anticipated going away for the long weekend. Maybe seeing Blue would help cheer him.

Immediately he spotted the little red vehicle she called a car parked by the barn. His heart beat faster, and he quickened his pace. He wondered when she had gotten there.

"You jus' miss her. She look like she want to be alone." Juan said from behind Trent at Blue's empty stall.

"Thanks." Trent crossed to Majestic's stall where he saddled his horse and left the stable.

He yearned for her to be there as he rode into the woods, not knowing if she would have taken one of the other paths. His anticipation grew as he neared the area. No longer his place—it was theirs.

His heart thudded against his ribs like horse hooves on hard solid earth as he entered the clearing. She stood facing the river. How he wished things could have turned out differently where Kevin was concerned. Nearly in a whisper, he approached her. "Maggie, I want to talk about last night."

She startled and faced him. "There is nothing to discuss. It's over, Trent."

"It doesn't have to be over. I know you went with him to protect me."

"I know the decision I made wasn't what you or my father planned, but I made it, and it's over with." She got back in the saddle and avoided eye contact with him.

"Every time you come here it's going to tear you apart. Eventually, you'll move Blue Bonnet from Rolling Rock. I don't want that, Maggie." He paused and waited for her to face him. "You don't need to protect me. We can fight him."

"Move on, and stay away from me where Kevin is concerned. It's not as if I'm blinded by what he does for a side living. I walked into the relationship knowing it...*and* him."

She turned the mare around and added, "Oh, by the way...you weren't the only one at the restaurant to get yelled at. Mike's here and doing business with Kevin again. Kevin had the balls to put me on display." Before she took off, she said, "It's over, Trent. Deal with it."

He would wait to see what transpired with Mike in town and then approach her again. Her father had talked with the DEA and now knew about Kevin. They had to be using Mike and watching Kevin. Maybe they would get him and lock him up, far away from Maggie.

~ * ~

Kevin enjoyed breakfast in the morning sun on the aft deck aboard his sixty-eight-foot yacht. The high-pitched whistle calls of the seagulls above the waters, floated on the slight breeze.

"Kevin?" Mike called, as he approached.

"Come on up," Kevin yelled.

Mike stepped aboard, and took the short set of stairs a to where he continued eating. "Nice boat. Business must be good ... in both fields."

"I'm doing well, but will be better once we see what you have for me. Would you care for some breakfast?" Kevin continued to wear his dark sunglasses.

"Thanks, but the hotel took care of me."

"Then let's get to business. Did you bring it?"

"Yeah, I've got it. You going to provide me with a little payment?"

Kevin smirked. "Now that's something we didn't discuss, but I'm sure I can find something to please you and your supplier. Let's see what you have."

Mike pulled the vial from his pocket and handed the vial to Kevin. "A payment would please my supplier more than you know."

Kevin checked the vial markings. "Looks like you have yourself a job, Mr. Nash. Let me go get you a starter payment."

Kevin went down to the master suite. Once there, he pulled the bedding back, lifted and pulled an envelope from the underside of the mattress. He counted the bills and removed the excess. Returning the cash under his bed, he returned topside. "There's three G's inside." Handing the envelope to Mike, he said, "You decide how to divide it between the two of you, but I'm glad to have you back with me. Two weeks, I want ten mil for another three G's. Can you do it?"

Mike's eyes widened. "Yeah, but you can have it sooner and more if you want. Remember my source has a stockpile."

"Okay, call me when you get into town and we'll discuss a meeting place. Maybe we could go to dinner. You know the three of us, Maggie, you, and I."

"I think she'd strike like a Praying Mantis. You might want to reconsider before making plans." Mike stepped off the yacht.

Kevin called, "Let me know when you get into town."

"Stop. Federal Agents. You're under arrest."

Mike was pushed onto the dock by an agent and two more agents jumped quickly aboard the yacht. Kevin ran for the helm of the boat. An agent jumped and tackled him to the floor. Twisting and rolling, he fought to get free. More agents joined the fight and Kevin stopped resisting.

"You set me up you bastard," Kevin yelled. "I should have known you were here for her."

"I don't know what you're talking about," Mike yelled.

"You fuckin' set me up."

"Go to hell, Kevin!"

"I'm not talking until my lawyer is present." Kevin ground the words as they escorted him off the boat.

~ * ~

Saturday late afternoon, Lady Antebellum's "Need You Now," played on Trent's cell phone. "Hello?"

"Trent, this a good time or should I call you back?"

"Tell me you're calling with good news, Steven." His pace quickened as he neared the house.

"Not good, but great news."

"They got him?" he asked with anticipation.

"Today. I received a call from Mike moments ago. I don't know any details, other than the DEA has Kevin in custody."

Trent sighed in relief. The bastard was out of their lives.

"The DEA won't release any information since he hasn't been formally charged yet."

"Does Maggie know?" He entered his office and sat in the closest chair.

"I was going to call her when I got off of the phone with you."

"Good. I'll finish here and head to her place." With a brief pause, Trent added, "I'm going to take care of her, Steven. You have my promise."

"Thanks. I'm going to make that call now."

~ * ~

Home from work, exhausted mentally and physically, Maggie filled the spacious tub to take a nice long soak. Immersed in calming lavender bubbles, the phone rang, startling her. Drying her hands with a towel, she picked up the cordless phone and prayed it wasn't Kevin or Trent. "Hello."

"I'm glad you're there."

"Daddy," she cried.

"Hey, honey, it's okay. Listen, I have some great news."

"I'm glad because I could use it."

"Kevin's on the road to prison."

"How do you know?" The bubbles sloshed around her as she sat upright in shock.

"When you went against the plan you left me with no choice but to move forward with the original plan. He worked with the DEA, and because of his cooperation, they got Kevin."

"He was here to help me? He wasn't here to go back into business with Kevin?"

"You saw Mike?"

"Kevin told me we were going out to dinner, picked me up, and when we got to the restaurant he said he had a meeting with someone. He had the audacity to put me on display in front of Mike. I couldn't believe it."

If Kevin sent Rick after Mike the last time, he could send someone after her for this new incident that put him in jail. Panic flooded her as though she were caught in an undercurrent.

"Honey, what's wrong? You should be happy to be rid of him."

"Daddy, he's the one who sent someone to the house in Texas, searching for the drugs. What happens if someone comes after me? And this time I'm not so lucky?"

"Honey, you'll be okay. He's in jail. He can't hurt you. I'm sure they'll limit his calls and visits to his lawyer only." Her father was calm, but calmness didn't come so easy for her.

"Maybe the lawyer's part of it. He could set it up for Kevin. Maybe that's why they could never prove his involvement when they came after Mike."

"Trent is on his way. It's over, honey. Relax and spend some quality time with him."

"Okay. I love you."

Afraid, Maggie quickly stood and dried. Dressed, she swept through the house double-checking that all doors and windows were closed and locked. She closed the blinds before turning off the lights.

The garage door whirred opened. Immediately she flashed back to

Texas and Mike coming home. Her heart raced, and her temples pounded. She stood frozen on the stairway. She heard the garage door close and the rattle of the doorknob turning.

"Maggie?"

"Trent." Racing down the stairs, she threw open the door and flew into his open arms.

"I love you, Maggie."

He held her for a moment before lifting her into his arms and carrying her into the living room.

"I need you tonight. Make love to me." About to speak, she realized he was headed for the guest room and nuzzled her face into his neck.

In the first room on the right, he delivered kisses to her lips. He set her on the bed and pulled back the covers while she tossed throw pillows on the floor. Slowly taking possession of her mouth, the only thing they heard was heavy breathing and their hearts beating against each other's chests.

He slid his hand to the hem of her shirt and she finished pulling it off, while he took her breasts one by one into his mouth. Suckling the first breast, both nipples became erect at his attention. His erection pushed at the seams of his jeans.

A moan escaped her when his hand moved to the apex of her thighs. Her breathing became more erratic. Together as one again, Trent was the one who moaned as she wrapped her arms tightly around him.

Maggie lay in his arms after making sweet, slow love. "It's over. It's really over."

"You're all mine now," he said with a nod.

"It looks that way, doesn't it?"

"Yup, and I'm not going to let you go anywhere." Trent leaned over and gave her forehead a kiss. "Join me at the ranch tomorrow."

"I can't. I work." She got out of the bed and wiggling her eyebrows playfully said, "I need to get some sleep."

He met her at the doorway, and they went upstairs to her room. Hearing the news of Kevin's arrest helped ease the tension.

Then there were her feelings for Trent. He no longer hid his but gave everything of himself for her. He revealed his heart when he had told her he loved her, and yet he hadn't expected her to return the words. He was so loving and understanding about her feelings.

Everything she wrestled to repress for the week came flooding into her heart, mind, body and soul. After Mike, she hadn't wanted another relationship. Trent had so casually moved his way into her heart. He pushed her at the right times, but with compassion. She couldn't fight it any longer.

She loved him. And she planned on telling him soon.

~ * ~

Maggie had changed his view of women. She'd positioned herself to protect him, the team, and Rolling Rock Ranch. The other women hadn't and wouldn't have done what she did. They only wanted his money. She didn't. Something he couldn't overlook. Last night as he'd fallen asleep holding her, he'd thought about marriage and the future.

He couldn't help but smile as he returned home. Maggie was back with him, and Kevin was on his way to prison. Things could only get better for the two of them.

Back at Rolling Rock, he worked on some follow-up paperwork for the business and returned phone calls. Caught up, he strolled to the stables.

"She's back with us, Blue." He nuzzled against the mare. "And I'm not letting her go again. You're a permanent fixture here at Rolling Rock Ranch."

Blue Bonnet whinnied as if she understood, and Trent laughed. It had been a while since he laughed. It felt good. No, it felt great.

He walked back to the house and stopped to check the boat. With everything ready for them to go Wednesday, it hit him. He walked so fast he nearly ran to his office.

After everything that happened between them, this would be a perfect way to get away. Who knew, maybe they could stay a few days longer to spend time alone.

Trent dialed the phone and waited.

"Maggie Carlisle."

"I want you to come with us Wednesday. I want you to be with me for the weekend. Maybe a few days extra. To be alone."

"Trent, slow down. I can't go with you. I'm working this weekend."

"Can't you switch with someone?" he pleaded.

"No, I changed my hours already to help someone else."

"Then I'm going to stay with you. Lance can drive. They can do it without me." He wanted to be with her.

"No! You've done enough. The team needs you. I don't want them to hate me because I'm keeping you from them."

"They wouldn't hate you. It's my decision. If I choose to stay, then I stay." They'd be upset at first, but if he told them circumstances, they'd understand.

"No, I want you to go. I'll be fine. Kevin's taken care of, and I have work. You need to be there."

"Okay," he said. "You win. I'll go, but I'm calling every night and coming back as soon as possible."

"I have to go. I'll talk to you later."

Trent let her go. She was right about being safe. He would be there for her tonight and every night before leaving Tuesday evening.

Chapter Twenty-Four

Tuesday night, home from work, Maggie walked into the kitchen and found it empty. For the last two nights, Trent had been there. Surprised at how lonely she felt, she picked up the phone to call and wish him good luck.

No dial tone. She checked the phone. There was no power, yet the base unit was still connected. "It must need to charge." She set the phone in the charging unit and searched the living room for the other cordless phone. Not able to locate it, she went up to her room.

The phone sat on the nightstand, and she grabbed it. Dead, too. As she approached the land line phone on the other nightstand, a door creaked.

Maggie turned in the direction of the sound and came face to face with Kevin. He had a black gun strapped at his side.

"Kevin?" She prayed a surprised dumb act would work, nervously moving closer to him. "Did you want to go out tonight?"

"No, I'd rather stay here." He spoke in a voice as cold as death as he yanked her against his chest. "I think it's time we take this relationship to another level."

She rotated in his hold to break free but without success. Doing the next best thing, she tried talking her way out of it. "Kevin, I'm not ready, and you promised me you'd wait."

"I've waited long enough. I don't think you made your cowboy wait this long, so why should I."

"Kevin, no. You don't want to add rape to your other charges. Would…"

"No." He thrust her onto the bed and pulled the gun from its

187

holster. "I don't think I would. That's why you're going to agree to have sex with me."

"Kevin, please," she pleaded, "I'll do *anything* but that right now." Her stomach clenched, and tears stung her eyes.

"You've already lied to me once and went to the police. No, better yet, make that the D–E–fuckin' A, Maggie," he shouted.

He took a few breaths. His voice at a normal level was tinged with menace as he said, "I'll tell you what we're going to do. We're going to take my car and go back to my place, where you'll think about how you want to end your relationship with Mr. Cowboy."

"Okay, but can I at least pack a few things?" She wiped the wetness from her cheeks, doing whatever possible to stall.

"Please do." At her dresser, he opened a drawer and snagged a piece of lingerie. "Make sure to pack a few pieces like this one." He held a red lace thong and brought it to where she stood by the bed.

"How did you get out?" She decided to ask questions to help calm her nerves and keep her mind focused.

"You needn't worry your pretty little head about that. Let's just say I'm a respectable citizen, with a lot of friends and money."

She walked toward the closet.

"Where are you going?" he asked indignantly.

"I need to get a suitcase to put my things in."

"I'm right behind you, so don't try and do something stupid."

With her suitcase on the bed, she took her time putting belongings in the bag. She kept an eye on Kevin and his whereabouts.

"Let's speed things up, honey," he said behind her in a sultry voice. Her skin prickled and crawled, sending a shiver down her spine. "Make sure you pack a swimsuit or two. You'll need one for where we're going."

She spun, seizing the window of opportunity, and nailed him square in the jaw with her right elbow. He fell to the floor. She made a run for the stairs, but he snagged her around the waist before she could get to the first step.

His breath hot on her neck, he pushed her ponytail out of the way and firmly planted a wet kiss on her neck. Her stomach roiled.

"Please Kevin, don't do this." Tears streamed down her cheeks as he pointed the gun in her face.

"Oh, we're going to do this all right." He took her arm and forcefully pushed her to the bed. "Finish packing and don't try any more stupid shit. I'm going to get everything I want tonight."

"Okay," she said quietly, opening her nightstand drawer. She wanted her prescription sleeping pills and spotted the pencil that sat on top of her notebook. In one hand, she gripped the pencil and in the other her pills. Within her peripheral vision, she located Kevin and rattled the bottle.

"What do you have there?" he asked approaching and stood behind her.

Memories of the horrible afternoon in her Texas kitchen flooded her mind. She'd had no weapon in her hand and no control of the situation. Tonight, was a different story. She would fight. Her breathing heavy and hands shaking, she knew what she had to do if she was going to survive.

The elbow hadn't worked, but the pencil could. She tightened her hold on the yellow wooden barrel.

"Sleeping pills." She turned and stabbed the pencil into the side of his thigh. Kevin hissed and swore as she forcefully wiggled it around in his leg.

"You bitch!" He clutched his thigh. As he gripped the wound, Maggie kicked him in the stomach.

"Call me what you want. I won't let you treat me this way." With all of her might she pushed him back.

He smashed into the banister hard enough to spill him to the floor, flinging the Glock out of his hand. She scrambled after the gun and got a solid grip on it.

Kevin grabbed at her, bellowing, "I'll treat you the way I want, bitch. And if you want to live you'll do what I say. Now give me the gun."

"No!" She refused to give up the fight. She'd given up once before. She wasn't about to do it again. He stood and reached for her hands again to gain control. With her firm grasp on the gun, their arms went up and down. Her muscles strained to fight his strength.

"I'm not giving up this time," she shrieked as they spun around the room.

Her breathing heavy and weakening from the fighting, adrenaline coursed through her veins as they headed for the closed patio doors.

"Give up. You can barely breathe. I'm stronger than you," he shouted.

She delivered one good push against his chest, and he smashed through the door, taking her along. The glass bit every inch of her body. She held on tightly as he grabbed her arm and fought for control of the gun. Arms and hands flailed as they scuffled.

Maggie planted her feet firmly, twisting to the left and quickly back to the right. She broke free, still holding the gun. She steadied and aimed for his chest.

Kevin went still and faced her.

"You don't have the guts to pull the trigger, bitch," he said, patronizing her.

"Try me," she said coolly.

At her words, he took a step toward her.

Maggie held the gun securely and pointed directly at Kevin. What he didn't know hurt him. Her father had taught her how to fire a gun when she was twelve years old.

"Die, you son-of-a-bitch," she wailed as he continued to stagger toward her. The reports buzzed in her ears. Her hands tingled, now numbed from the recoil after firing multiple shots.

Gripping the gun, she stood in shock as her body took control. Control of her breathing. Control of her emotions. Control of her heart.

~ * ~

On the freeway driving to the airport, Trent dialed Maggie's number.

"We're sorry, the number you have dialed is temporarily out of service. Please dial..."

He redialed and got the same recording.

"What the hell is going on?" He called her cell phone.

"Hi! This is Maggie. Leave me message, and I'll call you back."
Alarmed, he dialed 911.

"911. What is your emergency?"

"There is no phone connection at my girlfriend's house or on her cell."

"Sir, that is not an emergency. You need to call the phone company."

"This is an emergency. I think something has happened to her. Her name is Maggie Carlisle, and she was involved with Kevin Shaw. I think he's done something."

"Sir, do you know if he's made any threats to her?"

"No, but—"

"Sir, I'm sorry."

He hung up on the 911 operator. "Damnit! This isn't right."

He pulled up to her house fifteen minutes later. The house lights are on but no phone service? What the hell was going on? He entered through the garage and listened Nothing.

"Maggie? Where are you?" No response. "Maggie?" He ran through the lower level of the house.

"Maggie, where are you?" He took the stairs two at a time. When he hit the top step, he turned to find the bed a mess and a suitcase sitting open with clothing inside. Dresser drawers were pulled out haphazardly.

Panic flooded him as he took the final step. His foot slipped from under him. He grabbed hold of the railing and regained his balance. Droplets of blood spattered the wood flooring.

From the corner of his eye, the balcony curtains blew in, so he turned to the doors. Shattered glass spilled out onto the deck. "Maggie?"

She stood frozen. He glanced around the deck floor and saw Kevin lying motionless.

"Maggie, are you all right?" Carefully he stepped on the broken glass and approached her. "Maggie, honey, it's Trent. Relax and hand me the gun." He heard the police sirens in the not too far off distance.

No response.

He slowly slid behind her and spoke softly. "Maggie, I love you. Relax, and give me the gun." He reached around her waist and positioned his hands over hers. "Maggie, it's Trent. I'm going to take the gun from your hands."

Her body relaxed and released the tension on the grip. He took the gun from her and wrapped her in his arms.

"I'm okay. Cut up a little. I don't think Kevin's okay." It came out a near whisper.

"I don't care about him. I care about you."

She shook in his arms. Her head fell to his chest, and she cried. She lifted her head and gazed into his eyes. "I love you."

He saw it in her eyes, heard her say it tenderly through the screaming sirens and held her a little tighter.

"Sheriff's Office. Hands in the air. Don't move."

Trent dropped the weapon, and the officers immediately stepped through the broken door to recover it.

"He's the one you want," Trent said, tipping his head in Kevin's direction.

"Slowly, walk toward me with your hands on your head."

Trent and Maggie walked single file back into the bedroom.

"Down on the floor now."

~ * ~

The deputies took Maggie and Trent downstairs, separating them into different rooms for questioning.

"Ms. Carlisle, we need to take some pictures of your wounds," she heard a uniformed officer say.

Maggie nodded. Numb, empty-minded, terrified. Her body was not her own as shock like an earthquake rocked her world.

The uniformed officer instructed her to turn this way and that. Lift this arm then the other, all with a flash and click of the camera. Each time the flash shone in her face, Maggie tipped her head down to the side, embarrassed. How could she have been so foolish? She had let her guard down when she had learned Kevin was in jail.

"Thank you, Ms. Carlisle." The uniformed officer stepped away and out the bedroom door.

Maggie remained seated on the bed. Another uniformed officer walked in with a paramedic. "I'm Deputy Godson, and this is—"

"Hi, Erica," Maggie said somberly.

"You two know each other?" Deputy Godson asked perplexed.

"She works at the hospital. We see each other on occasion," Erica answered. "Maggie, I'm going to take care of those cuts you have. Deputy Godson, can you step from the room for a moment? Maggie, you need to remove your top so I can have access to the wounds. Deputy Godson will also be taking your clothing as evidence."

The deputy left, and Erica calmly said, "I'll get you cleaned up as best as I can. You don't appear to have much glass embedded in your skin."

"He went through first," Maggie said hushed.

"That would explain things." Maggie and Erica remained quiet during their time together. Finished, Erica said, "You'll want to keep the deeper cuts clean and covered for a few days. And, well, you know what you need to do. We need to get you some clothing to put on."

"There might be something in the closet."

Erica went to the closet and rummaged among the clothing, then came back with sweatpants and a tee shirt.

"Thank you," Maggie said shakily.

"Deputy Godson will talk to you now." Erica walked to the door.

"Erica, is he alive?" Maggie needed to know if she killed Kevin.

"I believe so. He was taken away by ambulance. You can ask the deputy if you'd like."

Erica stepped out, and the deputy entered. Maggie remained where she was.

Deputy Godson pulled a chair from the corner and sat in front of her. "I need to ask you questions now about tonight."

Nauseating spurts of adrenaline pumped through her veins to her organs with fear of being arrested. She shuddered at the thought of prison.

"Would you care for a blanket?"

"Please." With each pulsating heartthrob, the blood vessels in her brain pounded on her skull.

He asked someone to find one and bring it into the room. "How do you know Mr. Shaw?"

Maggie started at the beginning when she was married to Mike and leading up to when she met Kevin at the street party. As she told the story, they brought in the blanket.

"Were you two dating?"

She sat and hung her head. The violent thrashing inside of her body had subsided. Settling like a tree after a storm swaying back and forth. Back and forth. "I joined him on two separate occasions, and after those meetings I told him I didn't want to see him again. He kept sending me flowers and calling me. I told him I didn't want to talk to him. He came to the house and confronted me." The storm reformed, sending chills over her body and shook. "He said I had to make a choice."

"What kind of choice?" Deputy Godson asked, scribbling notes on a pad.

"A choice of stealing drugs for him at the hospital where I work or be his girlfriend. I chose to be his girlfriend."

"Did you invite him into the house this evening?"

Maggie raised her head and looked Deputy Godson dead in the eyes. "No," she said firmly with a raised voice. "He was here when I came home from work. He broke in." She stared back at the floor and swayed slightly.

"Can you walk me through how things happened when you arrived home?"

She told him everything she remembered.

"Thank you, Ms. Carlisle. Is there anything else we need to know about tonight or leading up to this evening?"

"My ex-husband was in town working with the DEA. It had something to do with Kevin, but I don't know anything about it. My father knows."

"Thank you. If you could wait right here, I'll be back."

Maggie pulled a section of hair forward over her scar, combing through the section repeatedly. What were they doing to Trent? The questioning process was cold and distant. She wished he were with her. Wished he could comfort her. Wished to hold his hand. Wished for this to be over with.

"Ms. Carlisle," Deputy Godson said opening the door, "we're finished in here unless you have any questions. Otherwise, Mr. Randall is waiting for you in the living room."

She hurried from the room and raced into Trent's arms. Gently, his arms enveloped her, and he kissed the top of her head.

"The DEA has been notified. We have no further questions for either of you at this time. Unfortunately, you will not be allowed to stay here this evening. We need to process the crime scene. Ms. Carlisle, do you have a place to go to?" the deputy asked.

"Yes," Maggie said and gazed into Trent's eyes. "Is Kevin...?"

"He's in surgery right now." The deputy answered her unfinished question.

"You have the numbers where you can reach us." Trent shook the deputies' hands. "Thank you for your quick response tonight, but how did you know to come and where? I called 911, and they couldn't help me."

"We received calls about a lot of yelling that sounded like a fight. We'll be in touch if needed," Deputy Godson said.

Trent walked Maggie out through the garage and stopped to grab the door opener from her car. He helped her into the truck. Inside and seated, she rested her head on his lap. By the time he pulled onto the highway, she had fallen asleep.

They arrived at Rolling Rock Ranch with the sun a thread on the horizon. Tomorrow he would ask Maggie to move in with him.

Epilogue

Maggie's spirit soared free as she left the courthouse. Two years had passed since she'd shot Kevin on the balcony. Today, with her head held high, she was free as an eagle. Unlike Kevin, who'd been found guilty of selling and distributing drugs and sentenced to ten years without parole, courtesy of the Florida State Prison.

During the preparation for trial, she'd finally learned where her bullets pierced Kevin. She'd hit him with three out of the nine bullets fired, one in the shoulder, another in the stomach, and one more just above his knee. The shot in the stomach had dropped him to the balcony floor. But he'd survived to take his punishment.

He still had to go to trial for breaking and entering and aggravated assault against her. The fire department would be pressing charges against him for the fire at the ranch.

The house on White Sand Key was up for sale. She couldn't enter without remembering the terrible events. The only good thing about the situation was, in the last two years she'd realized with more certainty how much she loved Trent.

After leaving the courthouse, she joyfully joined Trent, her parents, Chloe, and Chad at Crab & Fin for a celebratory dinner. The table cleared off, conversations continued as everyone checked out the dessert menu. Trent slid from his chair and onto one knee. Maggie's mouth fell open then quickly closed. What was he up to? There had been no signs of nervousness from him throughout the day or during dinner.

Then his words came. "Maggie, I love you. Your father and mother have given me their blessing, and we've been through so much. Will you marry me?"

The air was cool on her heated cheeks as the room fell silent, and the restaurant patrons witnessed the proposal. She peered at her parents through tear-filled eyes, then settled them back on Trent.

She cupped his face with trembling hands and fixed her eyes on the deep blue of his. "Yes. Yes, I'll marry you." She kissed him tenderly though he kept it short.

Trent slid the ring on her finger, Maggie glanced at it and then back at him. He captured her mouth with his, and the kiss was full of meaning and life, just as the future would be for them.

The ring had belonged to his grandmother. Made of two simple pieces of gold intertwined, the band represented two lives coming together, creating a circle with new beginnings but with no end.

About the Author

Born and raised in Minnesota, Jody remains close to home living with her husband of twenty-five plus years, three children and a cat named Holly. Growing up, she enjoyed reading V.C. Andrews' the Dollanganger series, starting with *Flowers in the Attic,* S.E. Hinton, and Stephen King to name a few. Today her tastes run across the board in fiction and nonfiction, in all genres.

She has traveled throughout the United States, to the Bahamas and Cancun, Mexico. Between watching her youngest son play soccer, maintaining one of many scrapbook albums, and her role as the COO of the Vitek household, she writes contemporary romances.

Visit and contact Jody at www.jodyvitek.com

www.ingramcontent.com/pod-product-compliance
Lightning Source LLC
Chambersburg PA
CBHW020431180626
46812CB00003B/1182